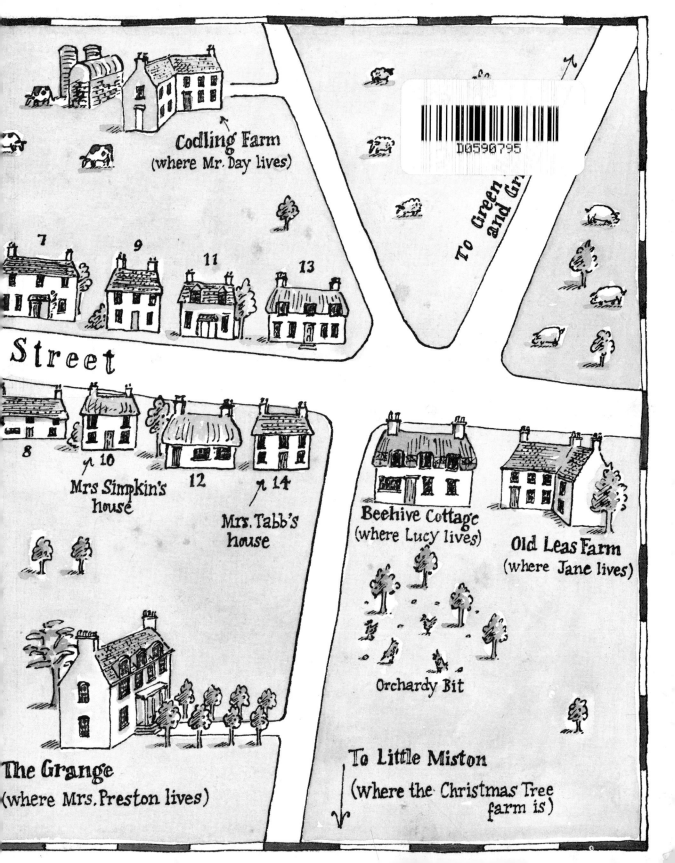

SUSAN HILL

Stories from
CODLING VILLAGE

Illustrated by Caroline Crossland

Julia MacRae Books   JM   *A division of Walker Books*

Also by Susan Hill

Novels
STRANGE MEETING
IN THE SPRINGTIME OF THE YEAR
I'M THE KING OF THE CASTLE

Autobiography
FAMILY
THE MAGIC APPLE TREE

Children's Books
I WON'T GO THERE AGAIN
SEPTIMUS HONEYDEW
ONE NIGHT AT A TIME
CAN IT BE TRUE?
THE WALKER BOOK OF GHOST STORIES

and many others

Text © 1990 Susan Hill
Illustrations © 1990 Caroline Crossland
All rights reserved
First published in Great Britain 1990 by
Julia MacRae Books
A division of Walker Books Ltd
87 Vauxhall Walk
LONDON SE11 5HJ

British Library Cataloguing in Publication Data
Hill, Susan, *1942-*
Stories from Codling village.
I. Title II. Crossland, Caroline
823'.914 [J]

ISBN 0-86203-455-8

Printed in Great Britain by
BPCC Hazel Books Ltd, Aylesbury

CONTENTS

1

Friends-next-door

One morning, Lucy Billings opened the door of the cottage where she lived, which was called Bee-hive Cottage, and went outside. She walked past her brother Ben's bicycle, around the corner and down the path to the gate. Just beside the gate was a wooden box set into the wall, and by standing on the old stepping stone beside it, Lucy could reach up and open the door of the box and take out the letters and newspapers that had been left there. (Frank, the milkman, put the milk for Beehive Cottage in the box too, but there were always five bottles, which Lucy couldn't manage safely, so her father or mother or Ben had to collect those.)

This morning, her father had taken the paper to work with him, but there were four letters and a small parcel and Lucy had just reached in and taken them out and closed the door of the box when she saw a blue car come slowly down the lane past Beehive Cottage, and stop by the gate of the house next door. There were two people in the front of the car, a man and a lady, and two children, a girl and a baby, in the back. And when the car stopped, the man got out and pushed open the big wooden gate of the house next door and wedged it with a stone, and then he got back into the car again and they all drove into the drive. For a moment, Lucy stared and stared after them. Then she scrambled down from the stepping stone and ran indoors, holding tightly onto the letters.

"Some people have come!" she said, and she almost tripped over the doorstep, she was so excited, "some people in a blue car have come to the house next door."

"What sort of car?" asked her brother Ben. He was cutting out a model from the back of the cornflakes box.

"I don't know what sort of a car. A blue car."

"What sort of people then?" asked Ben.

"A man and a lady and a little girl like me and a baby like Rosie."

"And a boy?"

"No," said Lucy, "no boy."

Ben made a face and went back to his cutting.

Then Lucy very much wanted to go back outside and see what was happening, because she thought that the people in the car had looked very interesting people indeed, so she hopped up and down on one foot until her mother said she might go, provided she put on her wellington boots, and Lucy didn't mind doing that in the least because they were brand new boots, red ones, and she was very pleased with them.

"Don't go out of the gate, mind," her mother said, and Lucy said no, she wouldn't because she never did, and Rosie the baby banged her spoon very loudly on the tray of her high chair and laughed and laughed for no reason in particular, the way she often did.

Then Lucy ran all the way down nearly to the very bottom of the garden, to where there was an open bit of fence, and climbed carefully up.

The house next door was called Old Leas Farm. A very long time ago, long, long before Lucy was born, there had been pigs in the pigsties and cows in the dairy and hens in the yard and ducks on the pond and sheep in the fields all around. But they had gone and the farm had been empty and tumbledown and the garden had grown as wild as wild, with grasses as tall as Lucy and nettlebeds everywhere.

Then, just after her birthday, which was in the spring, the workmen had arrived. They were called Bob and Steve and Alf and Gary and George, and they had been very nice, friendly, cheerful, whistly workmen, and Lucy and her brother Ben had often climbed up on the fence and looked over to watch them at work.

They had pulled down and cleared, they had hammered and sawed and drilled; a bulldozer and an earth mover and a cement mixer had arrived, and Ben had spent ages hanging over the fence every afternoon when he got home from school. Sometimes, one of the workmen had come to the back door of Beehive Cottage and asked Mrs Billings to fill their flask with hot water for tea, and Rosie the baby had sat in her pram and waved her arms at them or banged her spoon on the high chair tray and laughed and laughed and made them laugh back. She had laughed at

Bob the most because he always wore a blue woolly hat with a red bobble on the top and the bobble had bobbled about when he wagged his head, which he did every time he came, just to make Rosie laugh. But Lucy had liked Steve best because he called her funny names – nice-funny ones, like 'Princess' and 'Sunbeam' and 'Flower'.

Then one day Gary had come for the tea-water and told them he had a new baby at home, and that it was a little girl, and they had all said 'Hurrah'. And then he had said that he and Mrs Gary had decided they would call the baby Lucy, because he'd heard Lucy Billings's mother calling *her* so often over the fence he thought it was the best name of all for a little girl. Then Lucy Billings and her mother and Ben had said 'Hurrah' even louder and Rosie had banged and banged her spoon until the tray of the high chair rang and they had all put their hands over their ears.

But one day, Bob and Steve and Alf and Gary and George had finished working on Old Leas

Farmhouse and come to Beehive Cottage to say goodbye. Bob had given Mrs Billings a box of chocolates, to say thank you for all the tea-water she had boiled for them, and there were packets of fruity sweets for Ben and Lucy and some jellies for baby Rosie, and they had all gone to the gate to wave goodbye and Lucy had felt very sad, seeing their cars and vans drive away for the last time.

After that, the house next door had been empty and quiet all over again. Until today.

If she stood on tiptoe on the very top of the open bit of fence, Lucy could just see the back of the blue car, which was parked where the old pigsties used to be. But for quite a long time there wasn't anything else to see, and it was just beginning to drizzle a little bit of soft, drizzly rain onto her hands and her head, and she was thinking that she might as well go back inside, when out of the back door of Old Leas Farm came the little girl. She had plaits and a red coat and when she saw Lucy standing on the fence and looking at her she stopped, and looked back, and they both looked, and went on looking for quite a long time, until Lucy thought that any moment they might be

finished with looking and say something. But just as she felt that she was ready to, somebody called, "Jane! Jane!" and the girl turned and ran back. Only just as she went into the door again, she looked over her shoulder and Lucy thought that she smiled. So she smiled back. But then the girl was gone.

Lucy waited and waited and jigged about on the fence, but the other girl did not come out again and after a bit it began to rain hard and Lucy's mother shouted to her to hurry in. So she took one last look at the blue car and the empty yard and the tidy garden, before climbing carefully down off the fence and running back to Beehive Cottage.

For the next few days, Lucy asked and asked her mother about the people in the blue car. She asked if she thought they had bought the house next door and when they might be moving in and what their names could be – apart from the girl's name, which was Jane, she already knew. And Lucy's mother got very tired of saying, "I really don't know, Lucy," and, "You'll just have to wait and see."

Every night when Lucy went upstairs to bed she stood at the window of her room, which was at the very top of Beehive Cottage, and looked over at Old Leas Farmhouse and the empty yard and the tidy garden and the blank, dark windows and wondered and wondered. Some of her wanted it to stay empty and dark forever because that's how it had been ever since she could remember. Once, she had heard a fox bark from the garden there and Father said it had been on the prowl, just in case there might still be hens left, even after all these years. "Ghosty hens," her brother Ben had said and made Whooooo-whoooooo noises and flapped his arms, until their mother had told him to stop being silly.

When Lucy had gone to bed that night she had looked rather anxiously out of her window and over the wall, in case she might see the ghosty hens, and in the night she had woken up and listened and thought about the empty house and the yard and the garden, rather a lot.

But in the morning, when she looked again, she had seen that it wasn't frightening at all, but just the same, friendly-looking place she had always known, and cheerful, too, in spite of being empty and quiet. Only it seemed a bit lonely. Lucy decided that was what was wrong. And then another part of her very much wanted people to come and live in it and cheer it up and keep it company.

Nothing else happened for over a month, so that Lucy almost forgot about the people in the blue car and stopped asking her mother about them. And then, one Tuesday, something *did* happen, something very surprising and interesting indeed.

Every morning, Lucy went to the Codling Village playgroup. It was held in the village hall, at the other end of Codling Village from Beehive Cottage, and Lucy and her mother, with Rosie in the push chair, walked there and on the way they collected Sam Smith, who lived at Number 5, Codling, and took him to playgroup, too. Then, at the end of each morning, Sam Smith's mother brought Lucy and Sam back home.

On this particular Tuesday, it was a very leafy, blowy sort of day, with the wind rushing around and puffing into them, and the leaves swirling down from the trees, and Lucy had run about with Sam trying to catch them. Then they had both gone shuffle-shuffle-shuffle through all the piles of fallen leaves, so that by the time they reached Beehive Cottage, Lucy was feeling quite tired and ready for dinner, too.

Sometimes, Sam Smith and his mother came in to see Lucy's mother, and stayed for a cup of coffee. But today, the Smiths were going to town in Mrs Smith's old car, so they just saw Lucy in through her gate, and watched while she ran up the path and around the corner of the house and turned to wave goodbye to them. The back door of Beehive Cottage was open, and as she went in, she heard her mother say, "Oh good, here's Lucy now."

And there in the kitchen, sitting around the big table with her mother, were the lady who had come in the blue car to the house next door, and the girl with plaits called Jane. And sitting on the mat feeding each other with chewed-up crusts of bread were Rosie and another baby girl the same size, with curls like little corkscrews all over

her head, and a plump little cheeky face.

Lucy was so astonished that she stood stock-still and her mouth opened into an O. But then she felt suddenly shy, as well as surprised. Her own kitchen seemed to be so full of people she didn't know, and she went around to the other side of the table quickly and pressed very close to her mother and hid her head. Her mother hugged her and laughed and said, "*Now* you can find out what's going to happen to the house next door! You were asking me and asking me, remember? Well, this is Jane Jones, and her mother, and that's Jack Jones, on the floor with Rosie."

"*Jack* Jones?" Lucy said, and pulled away from her mother at once and went to stare at the baby with the corkscrew curls and the plump little cheeky face, and then everyone burst out laughing and Mrs Jones said, "Oh dear, Daddy was right, he *does* look like a little girl, we'll have to get his hair cut." And Jane Jones and Lucy both said exactly at the same moment, "Oh no, you mustn't!" Then they all laughed even more, and the babies on the mat looked up and saw everyone looking at them with laughing faces, so they both laughed too.

Lucy's mother said, "Well, I think that's broken the ice," which Lucy thought was a very odd sort of thing to say on a blowy, leafy, autumn-sunshine sort of day.

But then she said, "Do stay and have some lunch with us, won't you? It'll just be some soup and a sandwich," and Mrs Jones said thank you very much, they would like to, if it wasn't too much trouble, and Lucy saw that Jane Jones was looking and looking at her, so she said, "Can you do handstands?"

"No," said Jane Jones.

"Nor can I. Can you do cartwheels?"

"No," said Jane Jones.

"Nor can I. Can you go up very, very high on a swing?"

"*Oh yes!*" said Jane Jones.

"So can I. Let's go and do it."

So Lucy led the way out of the back door and down the garden to the orchardy bit at the bottom, where Mr Billings had fixed swings on to the branches of two old apple trees. They saw that lots of apples had fallen onto the grass in the wind that morning, so Lucy picked two up and gave one to Jane Jones, and they got onto the two

swings. First Lucy swung very, very high, and then Jane Jones swung very, very high, and then they both swung high together, and after that, they just sat holding onto their swings with one hand and munching their apples with the other, and the swings rocked gently to and fro.

"We're coming to live next door," Jane Jones said. "We're moving in next week."

And Lucy looked at her and smiled, and Jane Jones smiled back, and then they swung to and fro again and ate their apples a bit more.

Then Lucy said, "I've never had a friend-next-door before," and Jane Jones said, "Nor have I," and they smiled at each other again. And then, quite suddenly Lucy felt a great rush of happiness bubbling up inside her. She threw away her apple core and stood up on the swing and began to swing very hard and high indeed, and felt herself sailing up almost over the tops of the apple trees and into the sky and the wind blew her hair about and she shouted, "We're friends-next-door." Jane began to swing high standing up, too, and they both shouted, "We're friends-next-door," and laughed and shouted and swung in the wind, with the leaves and the apples falling all around them, until it was time to go in for dinner.

2

The Story of Queenie and Treacle

One fine Saturday morning, Lucy Billings heard someone calling and calling in the garden of the house next door. At first it was just one voice but after a few minutes there were two. So she ran upstairs to her bedroom and looked out of the window, and from there, she could see Jane Jones and her mother going up and down their garden and they were both calling and calling. Only Lucy couldn't hear exactly *what* they were calling and she very much wanted to know. So she ran downstairs again and out of the back door and all the way up to the end of the garden of Beehive Cottage, to where there was an open bit of fence. She climbed up on the fence and looked over the top and then she could see *and* hear. Jane Jones and her mother were looking, under the hedge and beside the hedge and in the sheds, and as they looked they both called, "Queenie! Queenie!"

over and over again.

Lucy knew quite well who Queenie was. A week ago, when Jane Jones and her mother and father and brother Jack had moved into the house next door, Queenie had come too, in a wicker basket with a lid. When Lucy had gone round with her mother to take a tray of tea and cakes for them all, because the electricity at Old Leas Farmhouse wasn't working yet, the basket had been in the middle of the kitchen floor, and it had been making a frightful noise, a sort of squealy-mewly-yeowly sort of noise. And when Lucy had bent down and lifted up a corner of the basket, there had been two green eyes and one brown and one black pointed ear, and a pair of white whiskers. Later, when all the doors were closed, Mrs Jones had let them open the lid of the wicker basket right up and there had been Queenie. She was a very pretty, very dainty, very small cat, and she looked as if someone had taken a brush full of brown paint and a brush full of orange paint and a brush full of black, and painted a bit of each here and there, just as the fancy took them, and then added a dab of white for luck.

"Not a proper tortoiseshell cat, I'm afraid," Mrs Jones had said.

"Not a proper anything," Jane Jones had said.

"In fact, a bit of a mess really," Mr Jones had said.

But then they had all said that they loved her just the same, and that was why they were being very careful only to let her out of the basket when all the doors were closed. Because Old Leas Farmhouse would be very strange indeed to Queenie, it would look strange and feel strange and most of all, it would smell strange, and she would be puzzled and very frightened until she got quite used to living there and had learned her way about properly.

"If we open the door now, and Queenie gets out, she'll just try and run back to our old house, and that's such a long way away that she'd be lost almost at once," said Mrs Jones.

So they had stroked and petted Queenie and then let her explore the kitchen. She had got out of the basket and sniffed and looked and sniffed and crept, twitching her whiskers and waving her tail, and occasionally just sitting down and yeowling a great, sad yeowl. After a while, Mrs Jones had put her back in the basket and closed the lid, and the basket had creaked and heaved about for a minute and then gone quite quiet and still.

"She's asleep," said Jane Jones.

So when Lucy stood on the open bit of fence and saw Jane and her mother going up and down, and heard them calling and calling, she guessed at once what had happened.

"Did Queenie get out?" she shouted to them. "Have you lost her?"

And Jane Jones said yes, they had. "And she's been lost since last night and we've called and called her and put out a dish of milk and we can't find her anywhere and perhaps she'll be lost forever and ever," she said, and then she began to cry, so that Lucy thought she must certainly not stand there on the fence but go and help look for Queenie straight away.

"I'm going to ask if I can come," she shouted to Jane Jones and quickly scrambled down from the fence and ran indoors. Her mother had already said that Jane could come and play at

Beehive Cottage for the morning if she would like to, and Lucy had thought all over again how very nice it was to have a friend-next-door.

So she rushed into the kitchen and said, "Jane Jones has lost Queenie, they opened the door and she got out and they're calling and calling but they can't find her anywhere and please may I go and help them look?"

"Yes, I heard them calling," her mother said. "Oh dear. Wait a minute and I'll come with you. But first we should really see if she's got through the hedge into our garden and is hiding anywhere here."

Then Lucy's mother picked up Rosie the baby out of her playpen, where she had been piling up plastic bricks and knocking them down again, and they all went outside and joined in the search.

They searched under the hedge bottom on their side all the way around the garden, and inside the tool shed and the wood store and the garage and the loft above the garage. They called and called and called, and in the garden of the house next door, Jane Jones and her mother went on searching and calling. And in the middle of it all, Lucy heard the whiny noise of Frank's milk float, so she ran down the drive to the front gate, where Frank was just taking out the five bottles of milk to put in their box.

"Hello, jam-pot, how are you today?"

Frank the milkman always had a different name for Lucy, and a lot of names were very silly; they were names like 'lettuce leaf' and 'tea cup' and 'cough drop', and they made Lucy laugh. But today she didn't laugh, she said at once, "Jane Jones has lost her cat Queenie, they left a door open and she got out and they've searched and searched and called and called and so have we but we can't find her anywhere."

And Frank said, "Dear me, I don't like to hear that. You tell me what this little Queenie-cat looks like, and I'll keep my eye open. She won't have gone far."

"She's brown and orange and black, all

mixed-up with some white bits, and Mrs Jones says she might try to go back to where they lived before and that's a very long way away."

"No, no, she'll be used to the new smells by now, and she'll know this is where she lives because her people are here, you see, and all the chairs and tables and rugs as well." And Frank banged the gate shut and climbed back into his milk float with a cheerful smile.

"I'll keep an eye open. We'll find little Queenie-cat, she won't be far away." And he winked at Lucy and off went the milk float, whiny-whiny, rattle-chink up the lane.

But Lucy wasn't sure, and a bit later, when Jane Jones and her mother came into Beehive Cottage, *they* weren't sure either, and Jane said she thought Queenie was lost forever, and began to cry again.

"Come upstairs and play, and I'll let you dress and undress Violet, if you like," said Lucy. Violet was her last-birthday doll, and still very special. So she and Jane Jones went upstairs and played with Violet, and after that, they did each other's hair and used Lucy's mother's slides and grips and hair combs to make themselves into grown-up ladies, and they almost – but not quite – forgot about Queenie, and Jane didn't cry any more. Only once she said, in the middle of pulling off Violet's petticoat, "But she wouldn't have come to your house because of Jessie. She's frightened of dogs." Jessie was the Billings family's big black labrador.

"Well, Frank the milkman said he'd look out for her, and tell everybody, and he said she wouldn't have got far."

"Oh," said Jane. But she didn't look very happy.

That afternoon, they all went in Mrs Jones's car to the park in Stillford, where there was a playground with slides and swings and a rope-walk and a roundabout, and a pond with ducks. Afterwards, they walked under the chestnut trees collecting conkers in two carrier bags. Rosie and Jack got out of their push-chairs and ran about and tried to find conkers too, but usually they brought back handfuls of leaves and a few stones

instead. The sun was shining and they all got quite warm and piled their coats into the pushchairs and then ran about a lot more, before going to the café in the park, where they sat at tables outside on the grass. They had orange squash and scones and jam and chocolate biscuits, and it was only when she was finishing her second biscuit that Jane Jones suddenly said, "But if she's lost forever, who will give Queenie anything to eat?" and burst out crying all over again. Her mother hugged her and said of course they would find Queenie in the end, they'd go home now, at once, and carry on searching.

"And Daddy will look."

"And *my* daddy will," said Lucy.

"Yes," said Jane, "and all the daddies in Codling Village."

And so they did. Or at least, a great many of them, and a lot of other people besides, because Frank the milkman had been around and asked them to. And Jane Jones's mother wrote out two notices on postcards. They read:

> ## LOST
>
> **QUEENIE**, our small brown, orange and black cat with white whiskers. If found, please return to
> OLD LEAS FARMHOUSE.

Then they walked up to Mrs Dobby's post office shop, and she kindly said she would put one of the notices in her window, and they pinned the other one on the village notice board by the telephone box. "There," said Mrs Jones, "now Queenie is sure to be found."

But she wasn't. Not that day or the next or the next, even though Lucy's father and Jane Jones's father went all the way down Magpie Lane to the fields and even as far as the wood, searching in the hedges and ditches with sticks, and Mr Day at Codling Farm let them go into his barns and hayrick and stables and cowsheds and outhouses to look, too. They said they had seen just about every other kind of cat there, because Mr Day had so many farm cats he'd lost count. But not Queenie.

On the fourth day, which was Wednesday, the most astonishing thing happened. Lucy and Jane Jones had come back from the playgroup, and they were playing in the outside yard of Old Leas Farmhouse with a lot of cardboard boxes and packing cases which had been used to bring all the Jones's things when they had moved, and which Mr Jones hadn't got round to breaking up or burning yet. They hoped very much that he wouldn't, because the boxes made excellent houses and railway carriages and tea tables. And in the middle of playing, Jane Jones happened to look round, and said, "Oh look, oh look! It's Queenie. Queenie's come home!"

Lucy looked, and there, walking daintily down the garden, came the little brown and orange and black cat, Queenie. And she was carrying something very carefully in her mouth.

"What has she got?" Jane Jones shouted,

"Oh, whatever has Queenie got?"

Just then, Mrs Jones came out of the back door holding Jack, and they all looked as Queenie walked towards them. She came right up to where they stood and then she stopped in front of Jane.

"It's a kitten!" Jane Jones said.

And so it was. A small, browny-yellowy coloured kitten. Queenie set it down very gently on the cobbles and gave a loud meowl, and the kitten looked up at them all and gave a meowl that was almost as loud.

"Is it *her* kitten?" Lucy asked.

"Oh no, it can't be," Mrs Jones said, and she bent down and stroked the kitten's head. "It's quite big – two or three weeks old, anyway, and we've only been here a week and Queenie certainly didn't have a kitten when we came."

"Then whose is it? Where did she get it from?" asked Jane and Lucy together.

But of course Mrs Jones didn't know. Nor did anybody else, though they asked all about Codling village, and even put up another two notices saying:

FOUND
One browny-yellow kitten.
Please claim from
OLD LEAS FARMHOUSE.

But nobody did claim him and nobody had any idea whose kitten it was either, and where Queenie had gone to for those four days was a mystery, too.

"I told you she wouldn't have gone far away," said Frank the milkman, when he heard. Only Lucy thought that she might have been, she might have been miles and miles and miles. But nobody would ever be able to find out.

Mrs Dobby at the post office shop was very glad to hear that Queenie had come home, but she wasn't a bit surprised. "That's cats for you," she said, "they just turn up when they feel like it."

But the oddest thing of all was that although Queenie had brought the kitten back in her mouth, and they seemed to be very happy together, what the kitten liked best was following Lucy Billings home to Beehive Cottage, and sometimes even to come to look for her when she was already there without Jane Jones. However often they took it back to the house next door, sooner or later it would just turn up again, so that in the end, Lucy's father said they might just as well give in and keep it. Only Lucy's mother said she wasn't so sure about that, they had quite enough mouths to feed as it was.

But one cold morning, they came downstairs in to the kitchen to find the kitten curled up with Jessie in her basket by the range, and after that, Lucy's mother said it looked as if the kitten had got its feet under the table. Which Lucy thought was a very odd thing to say.

Then her father asked Lucy what she wanted to call the kitten and said, "I think Turn-up would be about right, myself," but Lucy said you couldn't call a cat Turn-up.

"I shall call it Treacle," she said, "because it looks like that."

After that, Treacle usually slept in Jessie's basket, curled up together with Jessie. Only sometimes, for no particular reason, it went off and lived at the house next door for a day or two. But it always came back, and after a while, Queenie even came with it occasionally and wasn't frightened of Jessie any more, though she would never actually get right into the basket, like Treacle.

"They're a bit like you two, those cats," Jane Jones's mother said, one afternoon to Jane and Lucy, "living in each other's houses half the time!" Which was perfectly true!

3

Apple Chutney

At the bottom of the garden at Beehive Cottage, where Lucy Billings lived, there was an orchardy bit, with apple trees and pear trees growing. In the middle of the orchardy bit was a hen house, and in the hen house lived seven brown hens. Around the hen house was a run made of strong wire netting to keep the foxes out. But there was a gate in the netting, and sometimes, Lucy's mother let her open it, and then the hens would come trotting and cluck-cluck-clucking out, to peck and scratch and strut about in the long grass.

When Lucy was smaller, she had been a bit worried by the hens and afraid that they would peck at her with their hard little yellowy beaks.

But she was quite used to them now and not a bit frightened: she took down a panful of corn and scattered it about for them in the afternoons, and helped her mother or father to give them their food, which was called mash, and change their water. She could even carry a small basket down to the hen house and collect the eggs. That was what she loved to do best of all: she loved opening the door and smelling the henny-straw smell. Sometimes, one of the brown hens was sitting in the warm, dark inside of the hen house and made a gentle little cluck from its nesting box when Lucy went in, and she talked back to it in a soft voice. "There, girl," she said, as she had heard her mother do. "There, there, there."

So, one fine afternoon, she was very pleased indeed when Dr Wilkins called to see if there were some spare eggs that she could buy, and Lucy's mother said that Lucy might take the basket down to the hen house all by herself, and see.

The gate was open, and the hens were outside in the orchardy bit, but they didn't come running up to Lucy, because she had already been to get them their pan of corn just after dinner; they just went on pecking about – though they did look at her with interest, to see what she was going to do.

She lifted the latch of the hen house door, and went inside and the straw prickled her ankles and made its nice rustley-scratchy noise. There wasn't a hen on the nest this time, but when Lucy reached down, she found five brown eggs and they were still warm. She picked them up one by one and put them into the basket. She liked the feel of them, they were very smooth and dry and quite heavy.

Then she locked the door again and carried the basket slowly and carefully back to the kitchen, where Dr Wilkins was talking to her mother. She was saying that she had just been to Forge Cottage to see old Mr Bean, who had broken his leg in the summer, and been in hospital. Mr Bean wasn't just old, he was very, very old indeed, and everybody had been very worried when he had fallen going down his garden path, and his leg had been broken quite badly. But Dr Wilkins said he was doing very well indeed now, and his leg was 'mending nicely'.

"He wants to get it completely right again in time for the Christmas Party," she said. And then, because she could see that Lucy was very interested, Dr Wilkins told them that some of the people had decided that it would be a good idea to have a Christmas party especially for all the old ladies and gentlemen who lived in Codling Village. It was to be held in the Village Hall on the Saturday before Christmas, and there would be a proper sit-down Christmas dinner, and then an entertainment, with games and singing.

"They're having Father Christmas, too," Dr Wilkins said, "and everyone will take home a present."

"I think that's a lovely idea," said Lucy's mother, "but won't it cost a lot of money?"

"Yes, and we don't want our guests to have to pay for anything at all, so we're going to try and raise some money. There's to be a jumble sale and Mrs Preston, at the Grange, has said that she will have a Coffee Morning, with a raffle. If you can think of any other ways we might raise some money, just let us know."

And then Dr Wilkins paid for the eggs and said that she had better dash, because she had to collect her twins from the school bus at the cross-roads.

"Well," said Lucy's mother, when Dr Wilkins had gone, "I'd better look out something for the jumble sale. There's always something in the cupboards that we don't need any longer, but somebody else might want. Perhaps you and Ben could go through your toy boxes, Lucy, and see if there are any things you don't play with now."

"Yes," said Lucy, "and I'll go and ask Jane Jones and *her* mother." And she ran down the garden and climbed over the open bit of fence into the garden of the house next door.

But Jane Jones's mother said that they didn't really have anything for jumble, because of having only just moved. "We gave everthing we cleared out of the old house to the Boy Scouts, for *their* jumble sale," she said, "so I'm not sure what we can do. Can you two think of anything?"

So Lucy and Jane went back down the garden

of Old Leas Farmhouse and over the open bit of fence, into the garden of Beehive Cottage, and got into the swings that hung from the apple trees in the orchardy bit, and talked and talked, and swung and swung and thought and thought, until Lucy's mother came down to them, carrying two flat wooden boxes.

"Would you two like to do a helpful job? Will you pick up as many of these windfall apples as you can, and put them into the boxes? They say that it's going to rain later, and once the fallen apples get wet they'll go bad quite quickly."

So Lucy and Jane did. They poked about in the long, tussocky grass under the trees for apples, and laid them in the wooden boxes, being very careful to check that there weren't any wasps crawling on them first, and throwing away any apples that had holes in them, where the tiny maggots had burrowed their way through.

It was very good fun

but quite tiring, and after a time, their backs began to ache from all the bending over, and just as they thought they would simply *have* to stop and rest, Lucy's mother called from the kitchen for them to come and have drinks of milk and some biscuits.

And as they sat at the kitchen table, enjoying them, Lucy said, "What are we going to *do* with the apples? There are a lot."

"I know," said her mother, and she banged the iron down onto a pair of trousers, and then took it away again very quickly, so that the steam hissed up. (Lucy always enjoyed that – she pretended that the iron was a dragon, with smoke puffing out of its mouth.)

"It's a problem every time we have a good apple year. We can store some of the apples in the loft, but there isn't very much room. I shall make some apple pies and put them in the freezer. But there are always quite a lot left over, and I do hate to waste them. Perhaps I'll just put them in a box by the front gate, with a notice asking passers-by to help themselves."

"I know, we could *sell* them and give the money for the old people's Christmas party!" Lucy said.

But her mother said that although that was a very kind thought, the trouble was that everybody in Codling Village had too many apples this year. "So nobody would want to buy any of ours."

"What if we *made* them into something, and sold the somethings?"

"Well . . ."

"Oh, could we, please, *please?*" said Lucy and Jane Jones together.

"What do you think you could make? I don't mind helping a bit but it really ought to be something you can do all by yourselves, oughtn't it? Then it really *would* be your own way of making some money for the Christmas party."

Then they thought about it and thought about it. Apple pies and apple tarts and apple crumble were no good, because Lucy's mother would have to do so much of the work.

"Well, think of all the jobs you *can* do yourselves," Mrs Billings said.

So they thought and thought again, and Lucy's mother got a paper and pencil and wrote down a list of what they had thought and the list said that Lucy Billings and Jane Jones could:

Collect things
Sort things
Wash things
Weigh things
Peel things
Chop things (being very
careful with sharp knife)
Pour things
Mix things
Spoon things out.

And when she read the list out loud, they all looked at one another and said, "*Apple chutney*!"

Then Lucy's mother said that she had a lot of jam jars that she'd been wanting to use for something or other, to make some room in the larder cupboard, and she got out the recipe book and found the recipe for apple chutney, and made *another* list of all the things they would need to make it. This list said:

Apples
Vinegar
Sugar
Onions
Raisins
Ground ginger
Spice
Salt
Pepper
Lemons

Then Lucy and Jane went looking in the larder and found everything they would need except raisins – there were only two or three left, rolling round the bottom of the jar. But Mrs Billings said that she could do with taking Rosie the baby out for some fresh air. So they all got their coats and boots on, and on the way Jane Jones ran into the house next door, to ask if she might go with them, and to put on *her* coat and boots. Then they walked up the lane and through Codling Village to Mrs Dobby's post office shop, where they bought the raisins and another bag of brown sugar, just in case they ran out. When Mrs Dobby heard about the plans to make apple chutney, she said that if the jars looked really smart, with proper caps and labels on, she would take some to sell in her shop; she said that she would stand them on the counter and prop a special notice beside them, to say who had made the chutney and what the money was for. She also gave Lucy and Jane Jones and Rosie the baby a white chocolate mouse each, because she said they deserved it for their kindness.

So that afternoon, as soon as dinner was over, Jane Jones came round to Beehive Cottage and while Rosie the baby went down for her nap, Mrs Billings cleared the big kitchen table and the girls washed their hands and put on aprons (and Jane Jones had to borrow one of Lucy's mother's aprons, which was much too big for her and made them laugh, she looked so funny). And then they sorted and weighed and washed and peeled and chopped (being very careful with the sharp knife) and measured out and spooned in and mixed and mixed and mixed and mixed. Mrs Billings scarcely had to help them at all.

By the time they had finished they were tired and sticky and a bit hot, so they took off their aprons and washed their hands again, and then Lucy's mother said that while she put the chutney onto the stove to cook, they could go out into the garden to play.

So they did. They swung on the swings and then they played galloping horses with broomsticks from the shed. In the kitchen the chutney simmered and bubbled and the sweet-spicy-vinegary-appley smell of it seeped out through the open door, so that when Jane Jones's mother came round with Jack, a bit later, she stopped half way down the path and said, "*What* is that delicious smell?"

Later, when the chutney had cooked right through and then cooled on the window-ledge, Lucy and Jane Jones spooned it carefully, spoon by spoon, into the gleaming-clean jam jars, and stuck little waxy paper circles on the top. And Jane Jones's mother said that if they liked, she would decorate some plain white labels and write *Apple Chutney by Lucy Billings and Jane Jones* on them in her special writing (because she was an artist and could do painting and drawing and decorating with special writing, quite beautifully). Lucy's

mother found some spare pieces of red-and-white and blue-and-white cotton material in her sewing drawer and Lucy and Jane Jones drew around big cardboard circles onto the material and then cut them out with the pinking-shears that made frilly edges.

When the red-and-white and blue-and-white material covers were fitted onto the lids of the jars with elastic bands and the decorated and specially-written labels stuck on the front, the rows of chutney jars looked perfect. "Better than in the shops," said Lucy's father, when he came home.

"Yes," said Lucy, "and the chutney tastes better too."

Which everyone in Codling Village who bought it agreed was perfectly true. Because as soon as the jars went onto Mrs Dobby's post office shop counter, she started to sell them. And Lucy and Jane Jones also set up a stall, made out of one of the old packing cases, and covered with a tablecloth, between the front gate of Beehive Cottage and the front gate of the house next door, and Jane Jones's mother wrote out a notice about the chutney, and they propped it up in front of the row of jars.

That day was a Saturday, and the Billings family went off for the whole day to Fairleigh, to have lunch and tea with their cousins, and by the time they got back, it was dark. But there was a huge moon, and when their car stopped beside the front gate, Lucy could see the white table-cloth gleaming on top of the packing case – gleaming, and *empty*!

"It's gone, it's gone!" she said, scrambling out of the car. "All the chutney has been sold!"

"Yes," said her father, picking up the tin box they had left beside it, "the stall is empty, but *this* feels rather full," and he shook it and it rattled and then he gave it to Lucy to carry into the house.

"A lot of people come walking down this way at the weekend, especially when the weather's so fine," said Lucy's mother. "I thought it would be a good day to set up a stall."

Then Lucy poured the money out of the tin onto the big kitchen table, and they all agreed that big brother Ben should be the one to count it. So while Mrs Billings was putting Rosie the baby to bed and Mr Billings was putting the potatoes into the over to bake for supper, Ben Billings counted the money very, very carefully.

And he found that there was £11.50. And on Monday, Mrs Dobby said that she had sold out of the apple chutney that she had taken for the shop, and her money came to £6, which made £17.50 altogether.

Then Lucy Billings's mother wrote a letter to Mrs Day at Codling Farm, who was in charge of organising the Christmas Party for the old people, and explained all about the apple chutney that Lucy and Jane Jones had made. She put the letter, with the money inside it, into an envelope and delivered it that afternoon.

A few days later, Mrs Day wrote a letter back to Lucy and Jane Jones and said that the Committee had decided to use the chutney money to buy all the decorations to make the village hall look really pretty for the party, and for some boxes of Christmas crackers, too, to put on each side plate at the dinner; and she asked if, nearer the time, Lucy and Jane Jones would like to come with her to Stillford, to help choose the decorations.

And, nearer the time, that was just what they did.

4

A Very Special Birthday

At eleven o'clock every morning, Lucy Billings and Jane Jones and all the other children at the Codling Village playgroup, sat down and had a mug of milk to drink and two sugary biscuits. And one fine morning in November, when they were all nicely settled, Mrs Greene, who was the lady in charge, said that she had something special she wanted to talk to them about.

"Now I'm sure that you all know Mrs Tabb, who lives at Number 14, Codling. Is there anyone who *doesn't* know her?"

Jane Jones put up her hand, because she hadn't lived long enough in Codling Village to know many people at all.

"Well," said Mrs Greene, "Mrs Tabb was born in the cottage that she still lives in, the one at the very end of the row, next to the church path, and she was christened in our church and married there too, and all her children and grandchildren were christened and married there."

"Yes," said Lucy Billings, "and Mrs Tabb always sits in her chair by the window in winter, and in her chair in the front doorway when it's summertime."

"And she always waves to me," said Mark-by-the-pond (whose real name was Mark Field, only everybody called him Mark-by-the-pond, because that was where his house was, so as not to mix him up with Mark Cherry, who was called Mark-down-the-lane).

Then the others all said, "Yes, yes," because Mrs Tabb always waved to them, too.

"She waves to everybody," Mrs Greene said. "She is a friend to all the village. And something very special and important is going to happen to Mrs Tabb next Thursday, which is November the sixth." (And Sam Smith interrupted to say that November the sixth was the day after bonfire night, but Mrs Greene said that they would talk about bonfire night another time, because just now they were talking about Mrs Tabb.)

"On November the sixth it is Mrs Tabb's birthday," she said, "and it won't be just an ordinary birthday. Mrs Tabb is going to be ninety years old, and then she will be the oldest person in Codling Village."

She went on to say that because Mrs Tabb was a friend to all the village and to everybody in the playgroup, and because ninety was such a special age to be, they were going to do something special for Mrs Tabb. Next Thursday morning, they were all going to walk along Codling Village High Street, from the village hall, to Mrs Tabb's cottage, and they were going to go up her garden path, and stand under her window, and then they were going to sing to her.

"What will we sing?" asked Mark-by-the-pond.

And Mrs Greene said, "Well, what do *you* think we are going to sing?" and they all shouted, "Happy birthday to you!" so loudly that Mrs Greene had to put her hands over her ears! Then she said that yes, they would certainly sing *Happy birthday to you*, and that they would sing another song, too, and the song was called *Bobby Shaftoe*, and she told them the first verse. Which was:

Bobby Shaftoe's gone to sea,
Silver buckles on his knee.
He'll come back and marry me,
Bonny Bobby Shaftoe.

"We're going to learn to sing that," Mrs Greene said, "because it is Mrs Tabb's favourite song of all."

And when Lucy Billings asked her why, she said that Mr Tabb, Mrs Tabb's husband, had been a sailor who had gone to sea, and that *he* had been called Bobby.

So then Mrs Greene went to the piano in the corner, and they all gathered round her, and she played the tune of *Bobby Shaftoe* over three times,

and then Mrs Wood, who helped her at the playgroup, sang the words. And Jane Jones suddenly said that she knew the song already, she had learned it at her old playgroup, and one or two of the other children knew it, too, so they sang with Mrs Wood.

For the rest of that week, every morning, the playgroup spent quite a lot of time learning to sing *Bobby Shaftoe* and practising *Happy Birthday to you*, so that they could go to Mrs Tabb's house and sing the songs to her.

"But will we have to push the piano all the way along to Mrs Tabb's house?" somebody asked, and Mrs Greene and Mrs Wood laughed a lot and said no, it would be much too heavy and awkward.

"Mrs Wood's daughter Kathy will be home from college that week," said Mrs Greene, "and she's going to bring her guitar and play that for you to sing to." Which they all thought was a very nice idea.

And Lucy Billings and Jane Jones practised singing *Happy Birthday to you* and *Bobby Shaftoe* at home, every minute that they could (and so did all the other children at the playgroup) until in the end Lucy's mother said, "Oh, not *again*!" and

Jane Jones's mother said, "I think you know them quite well enough by now!" and Lucy Billings's father said, "Change the record, old girl," and Jane Jones's father said, "No wonder Bobby Shaftoe went to sea!"

But Lucy and Jane Jones (and all the other children at the playgroup) said they had to make sure their songs were quite perfect by next Thursday and that was why they had to practise and practise, because Mrs Greene and Mrs Wood had said so.

On the morning of November the sixth, Lucy Billings jumped out of bed and ran to her window and drew back the curtains and clapped her hands for joy, because it was a *beautiful* morning with a bright blue sky, and the sun just coming out, which was exactly right for a special birthday.

Though Mr Billings said that there had been a sharp frost during the night, and all the dahlia flowers had been pinched off by it, and Mrs Billings said that Lucy would have to wrap up really warmly, with her scarf and hat and gloves as well as her coat, because it would be chilly standing outside Mrs Tabb's house while they sang.

When Lucy heard the post van and ran down the front path to the gate to collect the letters from the wooden box, the post lady said that she had a very big pile of letters and cards and parcels indeed for Mrs Tabb's house. And when Frank the milkman came in his float, whiny whiny rattle-chink down the lane, he showed Lucy and Jane Jones, who were just setting off for the playgroup, a plant that he had grown himself in his own greenhouse and which he was going to give to Mrs Tabb for his present. And Lucy and Jane Jones hoppity-skipped all the way up to the village hall, they were so excited. "Almost as excited as on *my* birthday," Lucy said.

Everybody at the playgroup kept their coats on, and when they had all arrived, Kathy Wood showed them her guitar and played the tunes over to them, to warm up. Then they had one quick practice. Mrs Greene had a posy of dried flowers which she said were best, because there were not very many fresh ones about in November, and besides, Mrs Tabb would be able to keep this posy for always, to remind her of her ninetieth birthday.

And then they set off, two by two in a crocodile, with Mrs Greene at the front and Mrs Wood at the back, and Kathy Wood in the middle with her guitar. On the way they met quite a few people they knew – Frank the milkman again, and Mr Potter the vicar, and people going by in their cars slowed down when they saw them and tooted their horns and smiled and waved.

When they got to Mrs Tabb's house they walked up the path, and first of all Mrs Greene tap-tapped on the brass knocker, and Mrs Tabb's grand-daughter, Mrs White, opened the door and she looked very pleased and smiley. But she put her finger to her lips, to show them that they must

keep very quiet, because the singing was to be a great surprise. Then she whispered that she would open the front window so that Mrs Tabb would be able to hear them clearly, and while they gathered beneath the window, she went to fetch Mrs Tabb, who was in the kitchen at the back of the cottage, and sat her comfortably in her chair with three cushions around her. Then Mrs White looked out of the window, and nodded to Mrs Greene, and Kathy Wood went to the front, right under the window, and played the first few notes of music on her guitar. And then everybody began to sing. They sang as clearly and as loudly and as beautifully as they possibly could:

> Happy birthday to you.
> Happy birthday to you.
> Happy birthday, Mrs Tabb,
> Happy Birthday to you.

And then, after a little rest, they sang:

> Bobby Shaftoe's gone to sea,
> Silver buckles on his knee,
> He'll come back and marry me,
> Bonny Bobby Shaftoe.

And when Lucy Billings looked up, she saw that Mrs Tabb was standing right beside the open window, and leaning on the ledge, so that she could see them all, as well as hear them, and she was smiling and smiling and looking so pleased and so surprised. When they had finished, she clapped her hands a great deal, so they sang *Bobby Shaftoe* all over again. And some people who had come out of the other houses and were standing by their front doors, and some other people who had come down the High Street and were standing on the other side of the wall, all clapped too.

Then Mrs Greene said that they had all come to wish Mrs Tabb a happy birthday and many happy returns of the day, and that they had brought a small gift, and she wanted Lucy Billings, who had been at the Codling Village playgroup the longest time of them all, to come up and give the posy of flowers to Mrs Tabb.

Only Lucy took Jane Jones's hand and made her come up too, because *she* had been at the playgroup the shortest time and because she was Lucy's friend-next-door.

Then they took the dried flower posy and handed it through the open window and Mrs Tabb said, "Thank you oh, *thank you!*" and kissed both their hands (because she couldn't reach down far enough to kiss their faces!). And Lucy saw that as well as smiling and being very pleased and surprised indeed, Mrs Tabb's face had some tears on the cheeks – which she knew meant that she was really, really happy!

After that, as they were going away, Mrs Tabb's grand-daughter came out of the cottage with a tin of sweets and there was one for each of them "from Gran," Mrs White said. So they all went back down the High Street in the sunshine, sucking their sweets and feeling very happy and pleased, on Mrs Tabb's ninetieth birthday.

5

Mrs Simpkins

One Wednesday morning, when Lucy Billings woke up, she did not want to get out of bed at all. She felt like snuggling down under the covers and going back to sleep again, because her head was very achy and so were her legs and her eyes felt tired and burning when she tried to open them, and when she swallowed, her throat hurt. But the pillow was hot and lumpy and the sheets were crumpled up, and everywhere she lay was uncomfortable, so in the end, she *did* get out of bed. Only when she went along the landing to the bathroom, her legs were very wobbly and strange and all that she could manage to do about it was cry which brought her mother hurrying out of the other bedroom, where she had been getting Rosie the baby dressed.

"Oh dear," she said when she saw her, "Oh, poor little Lucy!" And she bent down and lifted Lucy up, just as if she were the baby, and carried her back into her own room and sat down on the bed with her.

"I feel hot and my eyes are all stingy and burning and my head aches and I'm wobbly all over and my throat is sore," Lucy said.

And her mother looked at her and smiled and said, "Yes, and you're covered in spots, too!"

"I want to see, I want to see," said Lucy, and slid off the bed. But her legs felt all funny and wobbly again, so Mrs Billings lifted her up and carried her over to the big mirror, and then Lucy could see that she *was* spotty, very spotty, with little, pink, pimply spots all over her face and neck and on her arms too.

"I'm not quite sure what you've got," her mother said, "but it's back to bed for you, Lucy Billings."

And she put Lucy into her dressing-gown, even though Lucy said that she didn't need it, because she felt too hot and prickly already, and sat her in the chair, while she made the bed, and changed the pillowcase for a nice, clean, cool one. And as Rosie the baby was singing and chortling quite happily in the cot in her own room, Lucy's mother helped her to climb back into bed again and then she ran downstairs and telephoned to Dr Wilkins, and got Lucy a jug of orange squash with some ice in.

When she came back upstairs, she said that Dr Wilkins would come and see Lucy later that morning. Which she did, and she said that Lucy had got a nice case of chickenpox and was to stay in bed for the next couple of days, and then to get up if she felt like it, but not to go to the playgroup for a whole week. Which, just this morning, Lucy didn't mind a bit, she felt so horrid she thought she would probably not want to go to the playgroup ever again. She just slept and slept and slept, and drank a lot of orange squash. Once or twice, her mother came up and gave her pink medicine and sponged her face with a cool sponge and put some lotion onto her spots to stop them itching. And then she went back to sleep again. And before she knew where she was it was dark outside her curtains-with-the-cherries on again, and she could hear her father's voice, as he came in from work.

The next day, she felt horrid, too, though she did think that she would like to listen to a story. But halfway through it, she fell asleep, and didn't wake up for dinner or tea. But when she did, she felt a bit better, only very itchy and very cross and out of sorts with everyone. But she said that she would like to have something to eat.

"You're on the mend then, Lucy Billings," her mother said, when she brought her up a slice of toast and honey and a mug of milk.

"I didn't want toast, I wanted bread and I didn't want honey, I wanted strawberry jam," Lucy said.

"Oh dear! You felt too poorly to be cross and contrary before. But getting-better-people are always cross and contrary."

"Why are they?"

"I don't really know. I suppose the bugs and germs have made them that way, just as they made them spotty."

"Am I still spotty?" asked Lucy.

Her mother said, "Have another look." And when Lucy did look in the mirror again, she saw that the spots had got bigger and spottier than ever, and that underneath them, her face looked very odd and floury white, and her eyes were dark as dark.

"I look funny!"

"Yes. But the spots will go away soon. Just so long as you don't scratch them and take the scabs off. And you'll be feeling a bit better by tomorrow. At least, I *hope* you will."

And when Lucy asked her why, her mother said, "Because tomorrow is a bit of a problem, Lucy, as it's Friday."

On Fridays, Mrs Billings went to Stillford to help teach cookery to the big children at Stillford school. And Rosie the baby went one week to Sam Smith's house and one week to Jane Jones's house, to be minded. Lucy went to the playgroup in the morning, and to Sam Smith or Jane Jones's house with Rosie, in the afternoon.

"But whose house will I go to tomorrow?" asked Lucy. And Mrs Billings said that she was afraid Lucy couldn't go to anybody's house, because of her chickenpox.

"One of the others might catch it from you and that really wouldn't be fair, would it? You wouldn't like one of them to feel as poorly as you've been feeling?" And Lucy supposed that she wouldn't. But she still wanted to know what was going to happen to her on Friday.

"I won't have to stay here all by myself, will I?" she asked. But her mother laughed and said no, of course she certainly would not.

"Mrs Simpkins has very kindly said that she will come in and be with you," Mrs Billings said.

"Oh," said Lucy, in a very quiet little voice. And then, "But she might get my chickenpox."

But her mother said no, Mrs Simpkins couldn't, because she had them when she was a little girl, a long time ago, and you couldn't get them again, and that as all her children were grown up and lived far away, they couldn't get them either, so it would be perfectly all right for her to come and be with Lucy.

"But I don't *know* Mrs Simpkins," Lucy said, only this time in a loud, waily sort of voice.

"Of course you do, and it is very good and kind of her to say that she will come and look after you."

And then Mrs Billings went off downstairs to get supper ready, and left Lucy with a fresh jug of orange and a new book to look at, from the Surprise Drawer. (She had two special drawers in her room; the Present Drawer, which was where they looked when they had to give a present to someone unexpectedly and they hadn't time to go to the shops. And the Surprise Drawer, which was full of nice surprises for special times, like when you were cross and contrary with chickenpox.)

But although the book was just exactly the sort that she liked best, and ordinarily she would have been very pleased and surprised indeed to get it, now Lucy Billings did not even open it; she just sat up in bed and felt cross and thought about tomorrow, and how she did not want to be looked after by Mrs Simpkins.

Now Mrs Simpkins was a very nice and good and kind person indeed, and Lucy knew perfectly well that she was, and really she liked her a great deal. But because of her chickenpoxy crossness and contrariness, she thought that she didn't like her at all; and also, she wondered what Mrs Simpkins would be like at 'looking after', when it was such a very long time since she had had any children of her own to do it to.

So, when Mr Billings came up to see Lucy and said, "Hello, old lady – my, you *do* look cross," Lucy said, "Well, I am cross, I am very cross," and when he asked her why that was, she said that it was because she did not want to be looked after by Mrs Simpkins and when he asked her why *that* was, she said, "Because she has got a tall head and I don't like it." But that only made Mr Billings laugh and then Lucy got crosser than ever and shouted, "Don't laugh, it isn't funny!"

After that, Lucy's mother came upstairs and straightened her bed up and gave her another spoonful of pink medicine and told her to go straight to sleep.

"Well, I'm not tired and I can't and I won't," said Lucy.

But two minutes later, she did. And when she woke up the next morning, the sun was shining through her curtains-with-the-cherries-on, and Lucy felt much, *much* better.

And because she was feeling so much better, when she remembered that today was Friday and that Mrs Simpkins would be coming to look after her, instead of being cross and contrary and saying that she did not know Mrs Simpkins and did not want her and did not like her because she had a tall head, Lucy Billings was very pleased indeed to think that she would have somebody new to talk to and she wondered if perhaps Mrs Simpkins might play a game with her.

So when her mother came in and asked how she was feeling today, Lucy said, "I'm much better and I want to see Mrs Simpkins," and that made her mother smile again.

Then Lucy got out of bed and went to the bathroom, and first of all she looked at herself in the mirror to see if her chickenpox spots had gone. But they hadn't, there were just as many as ever before, and they were still very spotty-looking spots too, and when Lucy looked even closer she could see that there were spots behind her ears and even in her hair. Only because she felt such a lot better, she didn't mind the spots half so much.

Then she had a wash and brushed her teeth and Mrs Billings found her a clean nightie, and Lucy sat in the chair beside the window while her mother put fresh sheets on the bed.

"You can stay there for a little while," she said to Lucy, "as you really are feeling better."

But when Lucy asked her if she could go downstairs and wait for Mrs Simpkins her mother said no, she wasn't as better as all that.

Then she found Lucy a new colouring book and fetched her crayons from the drawer and Lucy sat and began to colour in a garden full of flowers, while Mrs Billings was getting Rosie the baby up and washed and dressed. And all the time she was colouring, Lucy wondered and wondered about Mrs Simpkins, and wanted very much to see her, and thought of all the things they might do together while Mrs Simpkins was looking after her.

And she didn't have very long to wait at all, before she heard a ring at the doorbell, and voices in the hall, and in just a few moments her mother came up the stairs and along the corridor to Lucy's bedroom, carry-ing Rosie, and behind them was Mrs Simpkins. And Mrs Simpkins was carrying a bag, a large and very interesting looking bag with handles, and things sticking out of it.

Then Mrs Billings said that if Lucy went on feeling so much better, she could perhaps go downstairs at lunchtime, just for a while, and that Mrs Simpkins was to help herself to anything she would like, and make a cup of tea whenever she wanted to. And after that, she kissed Lucy good-bye, and went off in a hurry, to take Rosie the baby to Sam Smith's house and then to go and teach the big children at the school in Stillford.

When the door had closed and they had heard the car go off down the drive, and away up the lane, and the house was suddenly very quiet, then Lucy Billings and Mrs Simpkins looked at one another, and they both smiled big smiles. Then Mrs Simpkins said that she was so sorry poor Lucy had chickenpox, because *she* had had it when she was seven, and she remembered very well indeed what a nasty, horrid, itchy thing it was, and how it made you feel quite out of sorts.

"So I thought I would bring a few things along in my bag to try and cheer you up," she said. And she reached down and picked up her bag and put it on Lucy's bed.

"Now . . ." she said. And she began to take things out of it one by one. Then, for the rest of that morning, Lucy and Mrs Simpkins were very busy and happy indeed with what came out of the bag, so the time flew by.

First of all, there was Mrs Simpkins's crochet, all folded up carefully and neatly in a clean white napkin. There was a little steel crochet hook and a reel of fine white cotton thread and Mrs Simpkins was in the middle of making a beautiful crochet collar, which she said was to be sewn onto a dark green dress. She showed Lucy the collar, and

Lucy looked hard at all the little loops and knots and twirls that were the crochet and she thought that it was a very, very clever thing to do indeed.

"Well, I wondered if perhaps *you* would like to do some too," Mrs Simpkins said.

And out of the bag she brought another crochet needle, and another reel of white thread. And first of all, Mrs Simpkins made a chain of stitches herself, and then she gave the hook and the thread to Lucy and showed her how to hold them properly, and then how to put the hook in and out of the thread to make some new stitches in the chain. And very, very slowly, Lucy did it, though at first she got into a muddle and the stitches came undone, and then she got into a different muddle, so they got knotted up into too-tight knots.

But Mrs Simpkins just smiled and undid all the wrong stitches, and showed Lucy how to do the crochet all over again. And after a little while, Lucy managed to do first one stitch right and then another and another, until Mrs Simpkins said that she was doing the crochet "as right as right could be", and that she would show her how to do some different stitches, to join the chain together.

"And if you go on long enough, round and round, you will make a little mat," she said, which made Lucy feel very pleased indeed. Only just for now, she thought she would put the crochet down and have a rest, because it made her eyes and fingers quite tired.

So then Mrs Simpkins delved in her bag again and brought out six little wooden clothes-peg dolls, all dressed in scraps of different materials, and with wool stuck on for hair.

There was a grandma doll and a grandpa, a father and mother, and two children, a boy and a girl, and Mrs Simpkins said that she had a lot more at home, a whole shoe-box full of them.

"I make them all through the year," she told Lucy, "to use up my scraps, and then I give them to be sold at Christmas bazaars and summer fêtes." And Lucy remembered that her mother had said Mrs Simpkins was always making something for the bazaars. She knitted woollen toys and sewed lavender bags and covered coat hangers and crocheted mats and embroidered aprons and shoe bags, and she made Christmas decorations out of fir cones and tinsel as well as all the peg dolls.

So while Mrs Simpkins went down to the kitchen to make a cup of tea, Lucy played with the peg dolls on her bed cover. Then, after they had both had a drink and a chocolate bun that Mrs Billings had left for them, Mrs Simpkins read Lucy a story. But in the middle of it, Lucy went to sleep again, because she wasn't really properly better from the chickenpox after all, and when she woke up Mrs Simpkins said that it was dinner time, and that Lucy could get up and come down into the warm kitchen.

In the afternoon, Lucy did a bit more of the crochet mat and then Mrs Simpkins opened her bag again, and this time she brought out a lot of very funny things. There were some conkers, still bright and shiny-brown, and a box of pins and some balls of different coloured wools. Lucy couldn't think what they were for. But then Mrs Simpkins said, "Haven't you ever made conker furniture?"

And she began to push the pins carefully and firmly into the conkers by pressing hard on their heads with a bit of flat wood. She put in four at the bottom of a conker, one in each corner, and then she began to wind wool between the pins, and around them across the gap, over and over, until the conker began to look quite like a little stool. Then she stuck two more pins in the top and wound the wool between and around them, to make a back, and when she had finished, she set the conker down, and there was a chair!

Lucy wound the wool around the next one, and they worked away quite busily for a while until they had a row of conker chairs and stools and little table, too, which Mrs Simpkins said Lucy could put in her dolls' house if she would like. And by the time they had finished, it was time for another cup of tea. Over tea, Mrs Simpkins told Lucy about the toys her own mother used to make for her when she was a child, and then about the great cart-horses that her father used to look after, on the farm where they lived. And after that, she got out a pair of scissors and some coloured paper from her bag, and cut some little paper houses for Lucy to join into a street, and they were just deciding who lived where and whether or not there was a shop, when they heard the kitchen door open and the sound of voices, and Mrs Billings and Rosie the baby were home.

When they came upstairs, Mrs Billings looked at Lucy and said, "My goodness, Lucy Billings, you look better. You're quite pink." And when she saw the conker furniture and the paper houses and the peg dolls and the crochet, she said, "And haven't you been busy?"

"Yes," said Lucy, "but why have you come back so early?" Because it seemed hardly any time at all since they had left. And when her mother said that it was the end of the afternoon and time for Mrs Simpkins to go back to her own house, Lucy felt very sad and didn't want her to go at all, she had enjoyed the day so much and done so many nice things.

Mrs Simpkins carefully wrapped up her own crochet and put it away in her bag with the peg dollies for the bazaar. But she said that Lucy could keep the crochet that she had been doing, *and* the conker furniture. And then she fetched another, special peg dolly out of her bag, one that she had dressed up as a bride, out of an old lacy handkerchief. "That is for you to keep," she told Lucy, "to thank you for being such a very good companion all day."

Later, after Mrs Simpkins had gone and Lucy's mother was settling her down for the night, Lucy said, "Can I be looked after by Mrs Simpkins again one day?" and Mrs Billings laughed and said there, and to think that yesterday Lucy had not wanted Mrs Simpkins to come at all!

"Well, I like her very much and I do want her to come," Lucy said, "I want her to come the very next time I have the chickenpox," which made Mrs Billings laugh all over again.

And the next day, there was a card through the letterbox for Lucy from Mrs Simpkins, which said that she did hope that Lucy would be quite well again soon, so that she could come to tea at Mrs Simpkins's house one afternoon. "Because," the card said, "there are a lot of things we have to get on with together."

So, in two weeks' time, Lucy did go, and she

and Mrs Simpkins had tea, with bread and lemon curd and a home-made chocolate cake. Then they settled down by the fire to make conker furniture and do crochet, and several other things besides. And after that, Lucy Billings went quite often, and Mrs Simpkins taught her to knit, too, and said that Lucy was a very quick learner. And Lucy said that after her mother and father and brother Ben and Rosie the baby and Jane Jones, who was her best-friend-next-door, Mrs Simpkins was the person she liked the very best in all of Codling Village.

6

The Crib Baby

One Friday afternoon, when it was very foggy and grey, and Lucy Billings was feeling cross because she had the end of a snuffly cold, a knock came at the kitchen door. When Mrs Billings went to open it, there stood Lucy's playgroup friend Mark-by-the-pond, with his mother and his sister Emily, who was three. And Lucy was very cheered up to see them, and Rosie the baby was cheered too, and kicked her legs and shouted and shouted, until Emily patted her and said, "There, there, baby," just like a real mother.

And while Lucy and Mark-by-the-pond got out the brick box so that they could build skyscraper buildings, Lucy's mother put the kettle on and found the cake tin, and Mark-by-the-pond's mother sat down at the big kitchen table. She said that it was very nice to be asked to stay for tea, but that what she had really come with was a problem. She said that she and Mr Field had been invited to a wedding the next day, in a city quite a long way off, and that they really did want to go, because it was Mrs Field's best-friend-from-schoolday's daughter who was getting married. And they had replied to say that they *would* go. But then they had found out that children were not to be allowed at the wedding, because so many people would want to take them that there would be just *too* many altogether, and as the people who were getting married couldn't very well choose just a few children to go, they had sent round a card saying they couldn't have any children at all.

"Well, that would have been fine, and we quite understood," Mrs Field said, "and Mrs Wood's Kathy was going to look after Mark and Emily for the day. But now we've just heard that she has the flu and is in bed, and can't come after

all. Mark can go to Mark-down-the-lane's house;
they have very kindly said that he can stay all day
and for the night as well. But what about Emily?"
And Emily, who was playing mothers and babies
on the floor with Rosie, and trying to get her to
eat pretending-cereal off a teaspoon, said, "Yes,
what about Emily?" in a very waily sort of voice.
So Lucy Billings's mother said, "What about you?
Well, *you* will come and spend the day here with
us, won't you?"

Then Emily jumped up and clapped and danced about, and Rosie the baby laughed and clapped too, though of course she didn't understand what it was all about, she was just doing what Emily did. And then Emily said, "And bring a little bag with my toothbrush and pyjamas in, and stay the whole night?" Lucy's mother said yes, certainly, if Emily really wanted to and was grown-up enough, and Emily said that of course she certainly was. "I shall stay for all week and forever, I'm so grown-up-enough," she said.

Mrs Field asked if it was really all right and quite convenient, and Lucy's mother said it was perfectly all right, and would be great fun for Rosie to have Emily to stay. "And fun for Lucy, too," she said. She gave Lucy a very particular look, which Lucy knew meant that she was not to say anything otherwise. Because sometimes Emily Field could be quite a naughty child, though she was never really *bad*-naughty.

"Where will Emily sleep?" Lucy asked them. Her mother said they'd think about that later, but probably in the little bed in Rosie's room, and Emily said, "Yes! Yes!" and jumped up and down again, and then she wanted to go upstairs right away, at once, to see the room and the little bed.

So Lucy's mother took her, and Emily's mother and Rosie went too. But Lucy and Mark-by-the-pond stayed in the kitchen, building the skyscraper buildings in a very quiet and peaceful sort of way.

Now on the next day, when Emily was going to be staying for the whole day and night, other exciting things were happening too, and the most exciting thing was that it was the Saturday before Christmas. In fact, that whole week had been exciting already. First of all, the playgroup had done a nativity play in the village hall, to which the mothers and fathers, as well as other visitors, had been invited, and Lucy Billings had been the innkeeper's wife and Jane Jones had been an angel, and they had done very well, without making any mistakes, and everybody had clapped and clapped. The next day there had been the playgroup Christmas party, with jellies to eat, and iced cakes and mince pies and crackers and balloons, and everybody had worn a paper crown and played games.

Then Lucy Billings and Jane Jones, with their mothers, had left Rosie the baby and brother Ben and Jack with their fathers, and gone into Stillford in the car after it was dark, to the late-night-shopping in the centre of town. All the streets had been decorated with Christmas lights, in the shape of angels with shining silver wings and Christmas trees with glowing baubles, and the shops were like fairy caves, glittering with lights and stars and silver and gold, and piles of presents. And they had all gone to visit Father Christmas in the Ice Palace, which Lucy thought was the most beautiful place she had ever seen. Father Christmas had talked to them in a very jolly, friendly way, and asked them what presents they would like him to bring (though afterwards Lucy and Jane Jones decided that this shop-Father Christmas was not the same one as the real-life, Christmas Eve one, and their mothers agreed, and said that he was an ordinary man, dressed up in Father Christmas clothes).

So it had been a very exciting, getting-ready-for-Christmas week altogether. The big kitchen table at Beehive Cottage had been full of mince pies and sausage rolls and Christmas cake, and the kitchen table at Old Leas Farmhouse, where

Jane Jones lived, had been covered with special Christmas cards and gift tags and calendars and decorations that Mrs Jones made, and all sorts of parcels had arrived with the post lady, and mysteriously disappeared again at once. On Sunday, Lucy Billings and brother Ben were going to help their father get the roof rack onto the car, and drive over to Little Miston to the farm that sold Christmas trees, and choose theirs, to bring home.

But on this Saturday, after Emily had arrived with her bag and taken it upstairs and put it beside the little bed in Rosie the baby's room, they all put on their coats and hats and scarves and gloves, because it was another very cold, grey and foggy day, and set off up the lane and along the High Street, to the gate that led to the church. Lucy's mother and Jane Jones's mother and some other ladies were going to be part of Mrs Potter's 'decorating team' which meant that they would help fill the church with beautiful greenery and flowers and berries, all ready for Christmas.

And when they got there, most of the other ladies had already arrived, and in the middle of the church by the christening font, where there was plenty of space, were piles and piles of holly branches with scarlet berries, and long strandy bits of green ivy and branches of other dark green and yellowy-green leaves, and jars of fat white and yellow and purple chrysanthemums. There were also bunches and bundles of leaves and thistle heads and seed pods that were gold and silver, because Jane Jones's mother had sprayed them with special paint.

All the electric heaters inside the church had been switched on, but it was still a bit shivery-cold, so the children kept on their coats and gloves and scarves (but they took their hats off, because Lucy Billings's mother said that was what you should do in a church). Then, while the ladies were all being busy with the decorations, Lucy and Jane Jones took Rosie the baby and Jack by the hands, because they could both walk just a little, and showed them round the church. They climbed in and out of the seats and took the nice bright kneeler-pads off their hooks and piled them up like bricks, and then unpiled them again and sat down on them, like stools. And Emily had brought Lucy's old dolls' pram, which Lucy didn't play with much any more, and she was very happy indeed, just pushing it up and down and in and out and round and round the church, with her dolly Grace inside it. So, all in all, they had a very good time.

Then Mrs Day called to them to come and look what she was doing. When they went to the corner of the church they saw that she had two very large wooden boxes, and that she was getting things out of them and unwrapping them, from old pieces of torn sheet, and she asked Lucy and Jane Jones if they would like to help her, provided they were very, very careful, because she said that the things inside the boxes were very old, older even than Mrs Tabb, and fragile – which meant that they could break easily.

And when they unwrapped and unwrapped,

and pulled off the old pieces of sheet, Lucy and Jane Jones found all the figures that went into the Christmas crib, made out of beautiful old painted-plaster stuff. Besides Mary and Joseph and the wise men and the shepherds and two angels with wings, there was a donkey, a cow, a sheep with a lamb, a goat, and a very small dog.

Mrs Day had brought a plastic sack full of clean straw from the farm, and they helped her to spread it out around and under the wooden stable and the manger and then to set the figures carefully, carefully in their places. And all the time, Rosie the baby and Jack watched, sitting in their buggies, because Lucy Billings's mother had

said they were better strapped in again just now, 'out of harm's way', while the crib was being set up. But Emily was trundling round and round and in and out and up and down with the dolls' pram, and didn't come near them once, only sang and talked to herself, and to her dolly Grace, until they had almost completely finished. Then she did come, and stood and looked, and said in a clear little voice:

"But there is *no* baby Jesus!"

And Mrs Day explained that there was but that he stayed wrapped up in the wooden box until Christmas morning, when he would be taken out and put in the manger. "Because that is the day he was born," she said.

"Yes," said Emily, "Christmas Day is his birthday."

But then she said that she wanted to see the baby Jesus doll even so, and her voice began to get very cross and whiny, so Mrs Day said that she would unwrap the figure, and they could all have just a peep. So they crowded round and saw the plaster baby Jesus, lying in his piece of old sheet, with his arms stretched out, and he looked quite like an ordinary, small, real baby, only more smiley, and with a bit chipped off his nose.

And Emily put out a little finger and stroked his cheek and smiled back at him, and was very, very interested, and helped Mrs Day wrap him back in his sheet and lay him carefully in the wooden box again.

Then one of the ladies called that there were drinks for everybody, and there was a table set up at the back, by the notice board, with thermos flasks full of hot coffee and chocolate, and beakers of orange for the children, and a plate of mince pies and shortbread biscuits too. So they all gathered round and had a church picnic, and admired the decorations. There were green leaves and red berries and chrysanthemums and gold and silver branches, on all the window-ledges and the altar steps, and around the pulpit and the christening font, and in big stone jars on the altar table. Later that night, some of the ladies were to come back and decorate the Christmas tree, when it had arrived and been set in place.

But Emily wouldn't come to the table and have a drink and a mince pie, she stayed by herself at the other end of the church, with the old dolls' pram, and Lucy Billings's mother said it would be best just to let her be, as she was 'a child with a mind of her own'.

Just before they left, Lucy Billings and Jane Jones went quietly back, to the corner where the crib was, and looked at the beautiful, still figures kneeling and the animals standing, beside the empty manger, which was all ready and waiting for the baby Jesus, and Lucy felt a very happy and excited feeling suddenly fizz up inside her, because now it was nearly, *very* nearly, Christmas.

Then they all went home, and it was quite dark, but the foggy greyness had gone and the moon and stars had come out, and the wheels of the two buggies and of the old dolls' pram went trundle-trundle down the lane.

At the front gate of the house next door, they said goodnight to Jane Jones and her mother and Jack, who was fast asleep, and went up the front path and into Beehive Cottage, where Lucy's father and brother Ben were waiting. And they all had sausages and chips and treacle tart for supper, and Emily played with Rosie the baby. Later

on, they had a bath together, which was great fun and a lot of noise and splashing for both of them, but nobody was a bit cross or bad-tempered or silly the whole evening.

But after Rosie the baby had gone to bed, and just a little while after that, Emily had gone too, and been tucked up in her little bed and kissed goodnight and read to, and after she had said that she liked it here so much she thought she would like to bring the rest of her clothes and toys and *live* at Beehive Cottage, and after she and Rosie the baby had both fallen fast asleep – well, then a very, very funny and surprising thing happened.

Mrs Billings was tidying up, and she said, "Lucy, would you be a good girl and bring in that old pram from the hallway, and I'll put it back in the shed later?" So Lucy did. And when she got the pram into the kitchen, she thought she ought to take Emily's old dolly Grace out of it, in case that got put away in the shed too, because Emily would be sure to want it when she got home. (Though she hadn't wanted to take Grace to bed with her, she only wanted her pink squirrel. "Grace must stay in her pram and be asleep," she had told Lucy's mother.)

So now, Lucy bent down and pulled back the bit of old quilt that was the pram cover, and there she saw Grace the dolly. And also *something else*. She saw, lying beside Grace, a bit squashed-in and half wrapped up in a piece of old sheet, *the baby Jesus doll from the church crib*!

"Oh look, look! Come and see what Emily has brought home in the pram!" Lucy said, and her mother, and brother Ben came. They all stared and stared, and for a moment none of them said anything at all. But Lucy had a very funny feeling inside, because she wondered what would happen, and if Emily had really meant to *take* the baby Jesus doll. But then her mother said, "Oh dear, oh dear!"

"But," said Lucy, "we shall have to take it back."

"Oh, of course we shall, I'll take it back first thing in the morning. I'll just pop it back into the box, that would be the best."

"And won't you tell anyone?" Lucy asked.

But her mother said that no, she wouldn't, because really, Emily was only just three years old and didn't quite understand what she had done, Mrs Billings was sure.

So that was what happened. Lucy's mother slipped up to the church very early the next morning, before the first service, and put the baby Jesus doll back, and nobody ever knew it had been away.

But a little later on, when Emily's mother and father arrived at Beehive Cottage to collect Emily, and she was saying thank-you for having me and going home with her little case, Lucy Billings ran and fetched the doll Grace.

"Look, you nearly forgot her," she said to Emily. "*She was in my old pram.*"

And she looked very hard at Emily, and Emily looked very hard back at her, and they went on looking for quite a long minute. But then Lucy saw her mother making a frowny sort of face over Emily's shoulder, and she knew that the frowny face meant that she was not to say *anything at all* about what had happened while Emily's mother and father had been away at the wedding.

So she didn't.

Snowed In

One morning in January, when it was still holiday time, so there was no playgroup to go to, Lucy Billings's mother said, "I think we'll go to town today. I want to do a Really Big Shop."

Lucy was very pleased to hear that, because a Really Big Shop meant that they would drive all the way to the big supermarket on the road outside Stillford, and when they were there, Rosie the baby would ride in the shopping trolley, while Lucy helped to fetch things from the shelves and put them in it. Then, when Mrs Billings had paid the money and they had loaded their shopping into the car, they would all go back and have a drink and a sticky currant bun in the supermarket café.

So that is what they did. They had so much shopping that Lucy's mother said she wondered if there would be room for them to squeeze back in the car again. They had bought such a great many things because they had run out of nearly everything after Christmas, and because Mrs Billings didn't want to have to come to the big supermarket again for quite a long time, she wanted to make her marmalade instead.

But they all *did* manage to squeeze back into the car, though they were very squashed up next to the cardboard boxes and bags full of cat food and dog food and washing powder and biscuits and flour and sugar and tea and soap and orange juice and cooking oil and baked beans and butter and salt and spaghetti and cheese and vinegar. Lucy thought that it wasn't really very exciting shopping, not like the shopping they had done before Christmas. But she could see that you couldn't have that all the time, and in a way, she decided that it was nice to be back to the ordinary-everyday.

So she sat in the back of the car next to Rosie the baby, who was strapped into her special seat, and they ate a ginger biscuit each, to help pass the time. Then Lucy played 'Round and round the garden, like a teddy bear' on Rosie's hand, and 'This little piggy went to market' on her toes (because Rosie the baby always took her shoes and socks off in the car) and Rosie laughed and

chuckled and kicked her legs and they had a fine
time, until they got far past the town and off the
big main road and right out into the country.
Then Rosie went fast asleep quite suddenly, and
that made Lucy feel tired, too, and want to be at
home by the fire.

Mrs Billings said, "Goodness me, just look at
that sky!" Lucy looked out of the car window and
saw that they were just climbing the big hill past
the wood, so that in a few minutes more they
would be in Codling Village. There was always a
lot of sky to see here. Lucy thought it was a bit like
being under a pudding bowl that someone had
turned upside down; and sometimes, when it was
windy, she and brother Ben came up here with
Mr Billings to fly the red and green kite with the
long, long tail.

Only now, Lucy could see that the sky was very, very dark – not dark with the night coming on, but dark with thick dark clouds. So she said, "I think it is going to rain in a minute."

But Mrs Billings said, "I don't think it's going to rain, *I* think it's going to snow! Those are big fat snow clouds."

"Snow!" Lucy said, and felt very excited, because it was more than a whole year since it had snowed; it was when Rosie the baby had been Rosie the tiny baby, and Lucy and brother Ben had made a snowman in the garden, and a snow house, too, a round one with a little door and a scooped-out inside that they could just crawl into.

"Will it really, truly snow?"

"Yes," said her mother, "I think that it really, truly will!"

And sure enough, by the time they got out of the car at Beehive Cottage the first few flakes of

snow were beginning to float down out of the sky.

But it was much too cold to stay looking at them, so they went in quickly and shut the door and Mrs Billings put the kettle on, and Rosie the baby woke up and was cross, so Lucy tried to cheer her up by making funny faces, and Jessie the big black labrador dog came up, all pleased to see them, so that they quite forgot what might be going on outside.

But later, when Mr Billings came home from work, Lucy saw that the sleeves of his coat and the top of his head had snow on them. And when she was going to bed, she looked out of the window of her room at the top of the house, and saw that the window-ledge was white and that the sky was full of pale, swirly flakes of snow. There were so many and they were coming so fast that they muddled up and danced about in front of her. And when she got into bed and had had her story, and her mother had turned the light off, she could still see the white, swirly flakes, even when she shut her eyes tight.

Mrs Billings said, "I think it's a very good job indeed that we did our big shop today," and when Lucy asked her why, she said, "Because if it goes on snowing as hard as this all night, I don't think we shall be able to go very far at all in the morning."

"Why? Whatever do you mean?" asked Lucy.

"Because we might be snowed in," her mother said.

"What is 'snowed in'?"

"It means that there might be so much snow that it will all pile up down the lane and up the drive, and especially if it gets windy, and the wind drives the snow in great heaps and drifts to the bottom of our lane. We won't be able to get out of the path at all. It happened once before, when you were very small."

But however much Lucy tried to imagine just what that would be like, she couldn't, and after a short time, she was so tired that she gave up trying and went to sleep instead.

In the middle of the night she woke up and heard the wind blowing, whoo-whoooo-whoo down the chimney and rattling at the window and whistling under the door – because Beehive Cottage was a very, very old cottage and there were lots of cracks and gaps for the wind to blow through. Then Lucy remembered the snow and what her mother had said about if the wind blew all the way down to the bottom of the lane. She wasn't sure whether she was excited or frightened, so she pulled up her covers and slid further down underneath them, where it was warm and dark and cosy, and went back to sleep as quickly as possible.

When she woke up again the next morning, she thought for a moment that it must be summer again, because the sun was shining so very brightly through her curtains-with-the-cherries-on. But when she hopped out of bed and went to the window and opened the curtains, she said a little "Oh!" of surprise. Because the world outside was white. It was the sun, shining out of a blue, blue sky onto the whiteness that had made the light so bright.

There was snow, deep, thick, soft, bright, white snow, everywhere that Lucy Billings could see. Snow in a fat bolster along the window-ledge and snow on the roofs of the shed and the henhouse and all along the fence, and snow on the roof of the house next door, where Jane Jones lived, and snow covering every branch of every tree in the orchardy bit of the garden, just as if Lucy's mother had piped them with icing, like the biscuits she had piped at Christmas.

Then Lucy ran downstairs without even

putting on her slippers, and straight into the kitchen, where her mother was just lifting Rosie the baby into her high chair for breakfast, and she said:

"It snowed! It really and truly snowed!"

Just at that moment, Lucy's father opened the back door and banged his boots on the step to knock the snow off them. Then he came inside and said, "Yes, it *has* really and truly snowed and we are really and truly snowed in!"

But then Lucy's mother said to hush because she wanted to listen to what they were saying on the radio, and she turned it up louder, so that they could all hear the radio man telling them about the snow, and which roads were closed and which buses were not running, and then, which villages were quite cut off. And after a minute he said:

"Little Miston" (which was near), "Griffield" (which was much nearer), "Green Hampton" (which was the village right next door). And then he said, "Codling Village."

Lucy jumped up and down and shouted, "Hurrah!" and brother Ben waved both his arms in the air above his head, and Rosie the baby banged and banged her spoon on the tray of her

high chair. And Lucy's mother said *wasn't* it a good job she'd done the Really Big Shop the day before, so that now they could all have porridge!

And they did, big bowls of creamy porridge with brown sugar on, and top-of-the-milk too, only they had to be rather careful with that and just have a little splash each, because Lucy's mother said that they couldn't tell when Frank the milkman would be able to get down the lane to them next.

And when they were all full of the hot, comforting porridge, and of toast and honey as well, Lucy's father clapped his hands and said, "Right, gang – work to do!"

So he and Mrs Billings and Lucy and brother Ben all got dressed in their warm outdoor things, and went outside (but Rosie the baby went back to her cot for her morning nap).

There were two big shovels for the grown-ups, and two small spades (which they had used in the sand on their summer holiday) for Lucy and Ben. And then they all began to dig a path through the snow. Only Lucy kept stopping, partly because it was such hard work, but mostly because she kept wanting to look around. She thought that the snow was so beautiful and strange, and that it made her own house and garden, and everywhere else as well, look quite different.

Mr Billings had already been out quite early and dug and dug, so there was a path through the snow, leading around the side of the house, and a little way down the front drive, and slowly, slowly the path grew and they got a bit nearer to the front gate. They hadn't been going for very long before they heard voices from the house next door, and the sound of more shovels shovelling the snow, so Mr Billings shouted out over the fence, "Hello there!" and a voice shouted, "Hello there!" back, and suddenly Jane Jones appeared, high over the top of the fence, because she was being lifted up by Mr Jones.

"We're snowed in!" shouted Jane Jones, and Lucy shouted back, "So are we!" Then they all went back to work. It took a long time, and Lucy's hands got cold and her gloves got wet and her back ached, so after a while, she stopped trying to shovel the snow, and just watched the others, and looked around. Once or twice she went back into the house to listen, in case Rosie the baby had woken up. And Jessie, the big black labrador dog, rushed up and down in the snow and bounded and bounced and snuffled with her nose and dug and dug and dug (but in all the wrong places, and not helpfully at all!) and had a wonderful time.

After a while, Rosie did wake up, so Lucy went inside with her mother to get her up. They dressed her in her red snowsuit and her wellington boots with the frogs on, and then they brought her outside and set her down on the snowy path. And she stared and stared and *stared*, and pointed and smiled, and looked at Lucy and then back again at the snow. And Lucy said, "Snow. That's snow, baby," and Mrs Billings said it, too. "Snow, Rosie – that's the snow."

But Rosie just went on looking and looking, and after a minute, she bent down very carefully and picked up some snow in her hand and

smiled, and she liked it so much that she picked up some more. But this time, she put her hand up to her face and began to *eat* the snow, and then she didn't like it at all. She made a dreadful, frowny face, and tried to spit the snow out and then to throw it away, and when she couldn't, but just felt it all wet and melty on her hands, she started to cry. So they took her back inside, and Mrs Billings said that perhaps when they had finished clearing the path, and the Joneses had finished clearing theirs, so that they could get through, they would all like to come and have a hot drink in the kitchen of Beehive Cottage.

So Lucy went out and called over the fence and asked them and they said yes, please, they certainly would. The path through the snow had reached almost to the front gate by now, so Lucy went down it and pushed through the piles of snow for the last little way, and just managed to climb onto the gate.

But just beyond the gate, where the lane dipped down, the snow was so high it was like a hill. And Lucy could see, as far as she could *up* the lane, that it was deep, deep, and rounded on top, as if somebody had piled up a lot of white pillows and cushions.

Then she said, "How will we get out? Will you have to dig with the shovels all the way up to the High Street?" But Mr Billings said No, the council men would come with the snow plough and clear the snow away, because it was much too deep up the lane for them to move it, and almost certainly right as far as the main Griffield road, too.

And he told her about a snow plough and what it looked like, and how it could make a path through the deep snow in just a few minutes.

"When will it come, oh *when?*" Lucy asked, because she very much wanted to see it.

But Mr Billings said Ah, that was the trouble, it might not be for a few days, because there weren't very many snow ploughs to go round, and they had to clear all the main roads first. It would take them quite a long time to get down to all the little side lanes like theirs.

So Lucy looked hard for a long time at the snow, and suddenly she wasn't sure if she would like being cut off for a very long time, and not be able to get out into the lane or walk up to the village, and to Mrs Dobby's post office shop, or to the playgroup, when it started again.

But just as she was worrying about it all, she heard a shout, and there stood Mr Jones with his spade, and snow all around him, right beside the gate. After a few more minutes, Lucy's father and brother Ben shouted too, and they had got the path through the snow all the way down to the gate on their side, so that all the Joneses could come in, though the path was very narrow and very slippery, and they had to walk very carefully indeed. But Lucy's mother said that she was going to sprinkle a lot of salt on the path, and that would melt the hard, icy snow, and stop it being so slippery to walk on.

Then everybody sat around the big kitchen table at Beehive Cottage and warmed their cold fingers on mugs of hot soup and told stories about other winters when the snow had come to Codling Village. And suddenly, in the middle of it all, Rosie the baby said very loudly, "Snow!" Only she wrinkled up her nose and blew down it at the same time as she said it, so that the word came out sounding very funny indeed. But still, it was quite clear, it was the word *Snow*.

"She said 'snow'!" Lucy and Jane both shouted out together.

"Snow," said Rosie again. "Snow. Snow." And each time, she wrinkled up her nose and blew down it as she said it. Then they all cheered and clapped their hands, which made her very excited and pleased, so that she clapped back, and went on and on saying, "Snow." Which was really very clever, because apart from something that sounded a bit like 'Mum, Mum' and something else that sounded a bit like 'Ben, Ben' Rosie the baby hadn't said any words at all yet. *Snow* was her very first really proper word!

Then the Joneses said that they had better be getting back to the house next door, and Lucy Billings's father said that *he* had better get on with seeing how the poor old hens were in their orchardy bit at the bottom of the garden. He said he thought he could get down there all right, because the wind had made the snow drift at the front of the house more than at the back, though it was still very deep over the garden.

And just when they were leaving, Mrs Jones said that she remembered she hadn't got any onions, and could Lucy's mother possibly lend her one. And Mrs Billings said that she certainly could, because of having done the Really Big Shop the day before, and did the Joneses need anything else, and they said that they had almost run out of washing-up liquid. So Mrs Billings fetched them a bottle of that, too.

Then brother Ben said that perhaps as they had got so much of everything, they had better pin a notice onto the gate post saying what they had to lend to anyone who had run out of anything. Which they all said would have been a very good idea, except that nobody would be able to get through the snow to the bottom of the lane, to read it!

"Besides," said Lucy's mother, "the snow plough will get through soon and Mrs Dobby will open her shop."

But the snow plough did not get through to Codling Village for three whole days, and by that time, a lot of people had been out with spades and shovels and cleared a path through to Mrs Dobby's post office shop.

And the very first person to get through to the village from the outside was not the man with the snow plough at all, it was Frank the milkman, going very slowly and carefully with his milk float, whiny-whiny-rattle-chink. He came slipping and sliding down the slope into the village at eleven o'clock on Thursday morning, and stopped outside the post office shop. But he couldn't manage to deliver the bottles of milk to every house, as usual, because of the snow, and so he took out all the crates and set them up on the path outside Mrs Dobby's shop. Then Mrs Dobby telephoned to two people, asking them to come and fetch their milk, and those two people telephoned another two people, until everybody in Codling Village knew that the milk had arrived. And when Mark-by-the-pond's mother telephoned to the Joneses at Old Leas Farmhouse, Jane Jones came down her own path and up the path of Beehive

Cottage, very carefully, and knocked on the back door, and told the Billingses about the milk.

So then Mr Billings went down to the shed and got out the old sledge, and put Lucy onto it, and he pulled her all the way up the lane and into the High Street, on the path that had been cleared through the snow.

Lots of other people were going up to collect their milk too, and they all called out to each

other, and said what would they do without Frank the milkman, and altogether it was a very jolly, friendly morning indeed.

Mrs Dobby's post office shop was so full and so busy that she said she was going to run out of a lot of things very soon. But Lucy Billings said that it was all right, because they had plenty of every-thing, after having done the Really Big Shop, so they could lend Mrs Dobby whatever she needed. Only Mrs Dobby said that was very kind of them, but really, she needed a lot more than Lucy's mother would be able to spare, and that she just hoped the snow would melt quickly now, so that she could go out and do a Really Big Shop herself!

But that night, just before she went to bed, Lucy Billings opened the back door and stood looking out at the snow. It was so soft and beautiful and silvery-white in the moonlight, and the air smelled so cold and smoky-sweet, and every-thing was so quiet and still, that Lucy thought she would like the snow to stay forever. But that if it could not be quite forever, then at least for a few days longer.

And it did.

Sheep and Shops

One Wednesday, when Lucy Billings's mother came with Rosie the baby to fetch Lucy from the playgroup, Lucy said, "What's happening today? Where are we going?"

"Well, I don't think anything is happening really," her mother said, "and we're not going anywhere, except home."

Which made Lucy feel rather cross, because nothing much had happened, and they hadn't been anywhere, for ages and ages, and the snow had melted a week ago and the spring hadn't come yet and summer seemed so far away it made Lucy feel tired just to think of it. And it had been a very ordinary sort of morning at the playgroup, with only the usual things to do, like colouring and painting and glueing, and only the usual toys to play with. Mrs Green hadn't even made any new playdough, they had just had to make do with the old, she said, until she had time, and the old playdough was going a bit dry and crumbly and wouldn't shape at all well. Even the story had been one Lucy had heard before. So, altogether, the whole morning had been very dull indeed.

"Can't we go in the car to town and do shopping and have a drink and a bun at the café," Lucy asked her mother. But Mrs Billings said No, they couldn't, because she'd been to the town to do all her shopping on Monday, when Lucy had gone to Mark-by-the-pond's house to play.

"Can we go to the playground then?"

But Mrs Billings said No, she was afraid that they couldn't, because it would be much too muddy in the field, and all the swings and slides would be wet because it had rained so much yesterday.

"Well, can we go to somebody's house for tea?" Lucy asked.

But Mrs Billings said No, they couldn't do that either, because nobody had invited them.

"Well, can Jane Jones come to play with me?"

But Jane Jones, who was walking home with them, said No, she couldn't, because she was going to Stillford with her mother and Jack, to have her hair cut, and then to see their Aunt Kate.

And just as she said it, they reached the gate of Old Leas Farmhouse, where Jane Jones lived and she opened it and ran up the path and around the corner of the house, while Mrs Billings and Rosie the baby watched, to make sure that she was safe. But Lucy wouldn't watch, because she felt too cross inside, so she stomped off up her own path, and round to the back door, by herself.

Then, when Mrs Billings and Rosie the baby came in, Lucy asked if they could have chips for dinner, because she thought that chips might cheer her up. But Mrs Billings said they were having tomato soup and ham rolls, which made Lucy crosser than ever because she thought tomato soup and ham rolls was such a very, very dull and ordinary sort of dinner.

"And *then* what can I do?" she asked, in a very waily sort of voice, "if we're not going anywhere and nothing is happening?"

"Oh Lucy," said her mother, "you are a cross patch today!" which Lucy didn't think was a proper answer to her question at all.

But when they were sitting at the table and Lucy was stirring her soup round and round and round in a cross sort of way, and Rosie the baby was leaning out of the side of her high chair to give bits of her bread crust to Jessie, the big black labrador dog, Mrs Billings suddenly said, "I know what we can do today, Lucy B. I've thought of something that is happening, after all. Today is the 'other Wednesday'."

"What do you mean?" asked Lucy, still in a very cross voice. But as soon as she asked, she had remembered. 'The other Wednesday' was library bus day, because it came and parked in the car park of the Codling Village pub, which was called The Cross Keys, every *other* Wednesday; and that was today.

"So when you've finished eating your lunch, you can go and find all your library books, and I'll look for Rosie's picture books, and put them all together in the hall. I'll have my cup of coffee and change Rosie's nappy and then it will be time to go."

So that is what they did. By the time Lucy had gone around the house collecting up the six books she had borrowed from the library bus a month ago, from the chairs and shelves and tables where she had left them, she was feeling much more cheerful. Going to the library bus was not the most exciting thing they might have been doing but she did always enjoy it and she liked to get her new books, very much indeed.

The library bus was orange, with blue writing on the side to say what it was, and a blue roof. By the time they had walked up the lane and along the High Street and down the hill to The Cross Keys, and met several other people carrying their library books on the way, the bus was just arriving. They all had to stand back and wait in a queue, while Mr Mee, who drove the bus, had backed it very slowly and carefully off the road and into the car park. Then they had to wait until he came round and let down the steel steps and opened the bus doors, before they could climb on board.

Mrs Billings took Rosie the baby out of her pushchair and carried her up the steps and sat

her down on the floor right at the back of the bus, where all the children's books were, and Lucy went with her and gave her an alphabet book to look at, and then she began to choose some stories for herself, while her mother queued to take the old books back and get their tickets.

And while they were there, Mrs Green from the playgroup came into the bus to choose her books, and said hello to Lucy and Rosie the baby. Then old Mrs Tabb's daughter came, and then Sam Philpot, with his mother. Only Sam Philpot was having one of his silly days, and wouldn't talk to Lucy, though he stuck his tongue out at Rosie the baby, which made her laugh and try hard to stick hers out back.

Then lots of other people came, and last of all was Lucy Billings's friend Mrs Simpkins, so that altogether it was rather like a party, inside the library bus, with the ladies chatting while they chose their books. Mr Mee and Miss Bolt, who was the other library bus person, chatted, too, and found the tickets and took the books and stamped them and gave them back again.

There were quite a lot of new books too, so Lucy took a long time choosing, and in the end her mother came and helped her. Then they both chose some for Rosie the baby, and Sam Philpot went on being silly and sticking out his tongue. And then suddenly, Mr Mee was ringing the little bell that he kept on the counter, to let them know it was time to hurry up, because the library bus would soon have to go on to the next place.

But when they got all their books together and Mrs Billings picked up Rosie the baby, and they were at the counter waiting, Lucy heard some very funny noises indeed outside, and Mrs Green, who had been going down the library bus steps, and Mary Cherry's mother, and Mrs Simpkins who had been in front of her, all came back up them again, and crowded into the doorway, saying Goodness gracious, *now* what shall we do, we can't get out! And Mr Mee asked whatever was going on, and Lucy Billings, who was quite small, squeezed between them all until she could see right out of the library bus door.

And from the top of the steps she looked

down and saw that the car park of The Cross Keys was completely full of sheep. There were dozens of sheep, all milling around and pushing each other and baa-ing and bleating, and nobody could get off the library bus because of them. And then she saw Mr Day from Codling Farm, and John Day, his son, standing out in the lane,

trying to get the sheep to come back to them. Their sheepdog Gyp was trotting in and out, but none of the sheep wanted to go the right way.

So then Mrs Cherry and Mrs Simpkins and Sam Philpot and his mother and Mrs Billings and Lucy and Rosie the baby and old Mr Pennyfeather, all had to stand in the library bus, with Mr Mee and Miss Bolt, and wait for the sheep to be rounded up by Mr Day and John. They talked and told stories about other times when sheep had got themselves into the wrong place, and herds of cows, too, and even, Mr Pennyfeather said, when he was a boy, a great fierce brown and white bull, which had got out of its field into the churchyard, one Sunday morning, while everyone was in church.

"Will we have to stay in the library bus all day, until teatime?" Lucy Billings asked her mother. "Might we have to *sleep* in the library bus?"

Mr Mee said that they did have two cups and a teapot and some milk and half a packet of biscuits, but there wouldn't be enough for them all, and that they certainly didn't have any *beds* in the library bus, so he hoped they wouldn't have to stay all day and all night. And in any case, the library bus had to go on to three other villages

that afternoon and they were already late for Little Miston.

Then there was a shout from the car park, and when Lucy wormed her way out again to look, she saw that at last Mr Day and John had rounded the sheep up, and they were all trotting out of the car park and on up the lane as meek as could be, and old Mr Pennyfeather said that was the thing with sheep, once you got their leader to go where you wanted, all the rest would follow.

And then they were all saying goodbye and laughing and chatting and climbing down the steps so that the library bus could get off to Little Miston. They could hear the sheep baa-ing and bleating away up the lane, and when Mrs Billings sat Rosie the baby in her pushchair, she began to make a baa-ing and bleating noise, too, and went on making it all the way up the hill.

They walked with Sam Philpot and his mother, but Sam still wouldn't talk to them or look at them and he wouldn't even walk beside them, either. After a little while, Lucy began to feel the crossness creeping all over her again, because the library bus had gone, and the sheep had gone, too, and it was just a dull, grey, ordinary day again. Though she did have six new library books, and Mrs Billings had promised to read two before tea and two after, when she had done some ironing.

When they reached the top of the hill, Mrs Billings said, "I've got to get a tin of shoe polish from Mrs Dobby's." And Sam Philpot's mother said, "And I've got to collect my bread. And how many people would like a currant bun, if Mrs Dobby has any left?"

And of course Lucy said that she would please, "And Rosie will because she always does," and Mrs Philpot said she expected Sam would like one too, only if he didn't stop being silly and start speaking to someone, he wouldn't be given one. And out of the corner of her eye, Lucy saw that Sam, who was hitting the hedge with a stick as they went along, was also smiling a very secret and wicked sort of smile to himself. But just at that moment, they arrived at Mrs Dobby's post office shop, and Mrs Billings and Mrs Philpot both said, "Oh dear!" at exactly the same moment. Mrs Billings went a bit closer to the shop door to have a look, and said, "Whatever can be wrong?" and she pointed to a large notice.

"What is it?" asked Lucy. "What's the matter? What does it say?"

"It says, 'Closed'," her mother read out, " 'Owing to illness. D.A. Dobby'."

"But Mrs Dobby is never closed," Lucy said. "Except for dinner and at night and on Sundays."

Sam Philpot went and pressed his nose up against the glass window of the shop and stared and stared in, and so did Lucy. But it was quite true, Mrs Dobby was closed as closed could be, with the board up in front of the post office counter and all the lights off.

"No currant buns then," said Sam Philpot in a very sad and mournful sort of way.

"No," said Lucy, "no buns." Which made Rosie the baby say, "Buns, buns, buns" over and over again.

"No," said Lucy, "no buns, baby."

"No buns," Rosie the baby said, then, "No

buns, no buns,'' until she made herself cry. Then Mrs Billings said, Well, they couldn't do anything about it because the shop was closed and that was that. And they turned around to go on home. But just as they did, a car pulled up beside them and Mr Potter the vicar got out. But when they told him that it was no use going to the shop, because it was closed, he said he knew already, and that he had just been to see poor Mrs Dobby in the hospital, and now he was going into her house to collect one or two things she needed. ''Because I'm afraid that poor Mrs Dobby has to have an operation,'' Mr Potter told them, ''and she will be in the hospital for some time.''

''No buns,'' said Rosie the baby loudly, ''no buns,'' and she began to wail and cry, ''No buns,'' until Mrs Billings told her to hush, and when Lucy and Sam began to chant, ''No buns,'' together as well she got quite cross.

''Never mind 'no buns',,'' she said. ''What about poor Mrs Dobby? Think of her.''

So Lucy did think of her, all by herself in the hospital and being so poorly that she had to have an operation, and she was very sorry indeed. ''Once, when Mrs Dobby broke her leg,'' she said, ''her daughter came to look after the shop.''

But Mr Potter the vicar said, "I'm afraid Mrs Dobby's daughter Margaret went to live in Australia last year. They will send someone specially to look after the post office counter for one or two mornings each week but I don't know if they will be able to do the rest of the shop as well."

And then he bent down and pinched Rosie the baby's cheek very gently. "We shall have to do something to make sure you get your currant buns," he said, before he went into Mrs Dobby's house.

After that, there was nothing to do except walk on home, and the ordinary day went back to being ordinary again. Except that there was quite a lot, about the library bus and the sheep and Mrs Dobby, to tell Mr Billings and brother Ben when they got home.

But before they did, something very interesting indeed happened. Lucy's mother was just putting the kettle on for tea and Lucy was opening the cake tin and getting out the plates from the cupboard, when there was a ring at the front doorbell. When Mrs Billings went to answer it, there stood Mrs Day from Codling Farm, and when she said she had come to ask for help, on behalf of Mrs Dobby, Lucy's mother asked her in, and to sit down and have a cup of tea, so Mrs Day did; and when she had, Lucy Billings said, "But Mrs Dobby is ill, she's in the hospital. It says so on the door of the post office shop."

"Yes," said Mrs Day, "and that's why I've come. You see, because Mrs Dobby will be in hospital for some time, and then not able to work in the shop for a week or two after she gets home again, Mrs Smale will come over on three mornings in the week from Griffield to do the post office. But she needs someone to take over the grocery counter and the till. And because there really doesn't seem to be anyone who can do it all the time, we wondered if it would be a good idea to ask people in the village if they would take turns at serving, just for a morning, or an afternoon."

Then Lucy Billings looked at her mother, and Mrs Billings looked back, and smiled. Mrs Day said that there were already two people on the list, and she wondered if Mrs Billings could possibly be the third.

"Oh yes, yes, please. Oh, you must!" Lucy Billings said, jumping up and down. And when Rosie the baby saw her, she tried to jump up and down in her high chair, and shout, "Yes" too, and just at that moment, there was a knock at the back door, and Jane Jones came in with her mother, who was carrying Jack. So Mrs Billings got out some more cups and saucers and re-filled the teapot and Lucy Billings told them all about Mrs Dobby being in hospital.

"I know," Jane Jones said, "because we just went to the shop and it was closed, so we've come here to borrow some salt instead."

And in the middle of all the chatter, Lucy Billings heard her mother say quietly to Mrs Day, "What about Wednesday? That would suit me best."

So the very next Wednesday morning, Mrs Jones collected Jane Jones and Lucy Billings from the playgroup and took them straight up the High Street to Mrs Dobby's post office shop. She unstrapped Jack, and Rosie the baby, from their buggies, and then they all went inside. And when Lucy got up to the counter, the lady who was serving behind it, wearing a red and white stripy apron, said, "Good morning, Madam. And what can I get for you this morning?"

And Lucy Billings said, "Good morning. I'd like four nice big sticky curranty buns, please." But then, although she tried very hard not to, she burst out laughing, because the behind-the-counter lady was her own mother! Mrs Billings took the currant buns out of the tray and put them into a paper bag and swung the bag round to make little ears at the corners, just as Mrs Dobby did, and said that she had been very busy

all morning, and that it was great fun and she couldn't wait to have another turn.

"But not tomorrow morning," said Jane Jones.

"No," said Mrs Jones, "because tomorrow morning, it's *my* turn!"

And Rosie the baby said, "Turn, turn," and then, "Bun, bun, bun," and waved it in the air.

And then, just for a minute, Lucy Billings went and stood behind the counter of the shop and looked over it, and said, "Good morning, Madam, and what can I get for you this morning?" to Jane Jones, and Jane Jones had a turn at doing it, before Mrs Billings shooed them all out of the shop, and home to lunch at Old Leas Farmhouse, which was where Jane Jones lived.

And after lunch, Lucy Billings and Jane Jones ran down to the bottom of the garden and climbed onto the fence and sat there, eating their currant buns and Lucy thought they tasted just a bit nicer and stickier and currantier than usual.

And the next day, when they bought their buns from Jane Jones's mother at the shop, and ate them sitting on the swings at the bottom of the garden of Beehive Cottage, Jane Jones thought exactly the same thing!

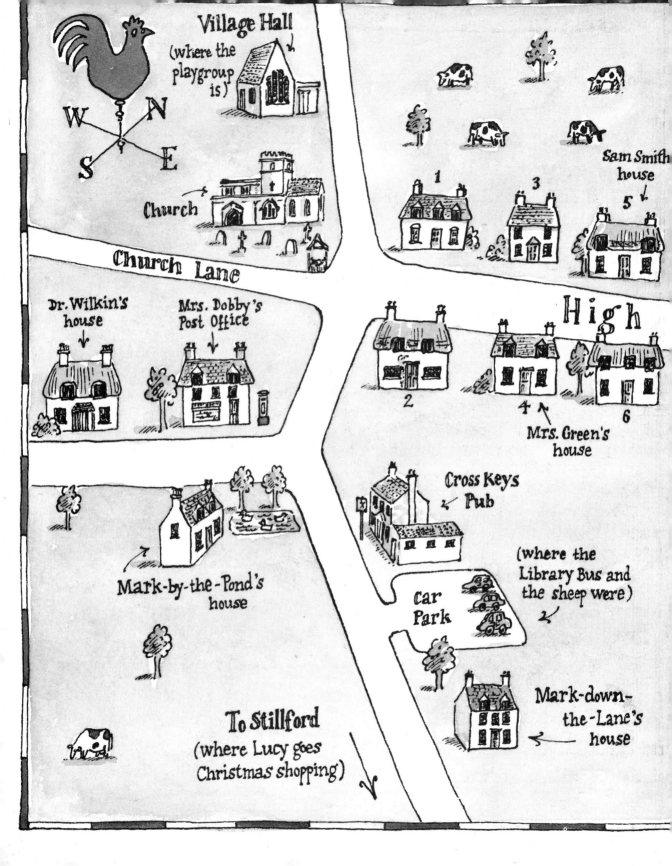